The Widow

Rowan S. Sterling

Table of Contents

Chapter 1 Maya's Return

Rosehill hadn't changed one bit. The sleepy little town still nestled among gentle hills and dense woods, a postcard-perfect image, if you didn't look

too closely. I'd spent half my childhood desperate to escape its quaint, suffocating charm. Yet here I was, drawn back by a death I hadn't anticipated or understood.

I parked in front of Aunt Eleanor's sprawling Victorian house, my house now, I reminded myself uneasily, and cut the engine. Silence rushed in, heavy and oppressive. My throat tightened at the sight of the wraparound porch, the rocking chair where Eleanor used to sit with her steaming mug, watching neighbors and scribbling in her leather-bound diary.

I stepped onto the gravel driveway, the crunch beneath my shoes

uncomfortably loud. The house seemed larger than I remembered, looming against the gray sky, its white paint chipped and peeling at the edges.

Memories flooded in: summers chasing fireflies, winters curled up beside Eleanor as she read by the fireplace. Nostalgia pressed painfully against my chest, but grief felt distant, tangled in confusion and unanswered questions.

As I climbed the porch steps, my phone buzzed in my pocket, startling me. I pulled it out and saw my editor's name blinking urgently.

"Hey, Margot." My voice echoed off the wooden porch ceiling, hollow.

"How are you holding up, Maya?" Margot asked, her tone cautiously sympathetic.

"Managing," I replied vaguely. "Just arrived at the house."

There was a pause, then, "Take the time you need. But remember, a story's a story. If anything feels... off, trust your instincts."

I sighed, glancing at the empty street. "You think there's something more?"

"Always," Margot said firmly. "Especially in places like Rosehill. Call me if you need anything."

I ended the call and stared at the brass key in my hand. The front door opened with a reluctant creak. Inside, the house was dim, the air thick with the scent of lavender and old books. Dust motes danced in pale beams of light through lace curtains. Everything was just as Eleanor had left it, untouched, pristine, as if she expected to return any moment.

I set my bags in the foyer, my footsteps echoing eerily. In the parlor, Eleanor's armchair sat facing the empty fireplace. On the side table lay her diary, worn and familiar. My fingers hovered uncertainly over it.

"Hello?" a voice called from the doorway, making my pulse spike.

I turned sharply. A middle-aged woman stood there, friendly but guarded. She wore gardening gloves and a faded floral dress, gray-blonde hair

pulled into a neat bun. "Maya Carter?" she asked gently, stepping forward.

"Yes," I replied, recognizing her faintly. "I'm sorry, do I know you?"

She smiled softly. "Mrs. Graham, dear. From next door. You probably don't remember me. You left Rosehill so young."

A flicker of recognition sparked. "Of course. Eleanor mentioned you often." Her smile tightened, eyes shifting uneasily. "I'm sorry about your aunt.

Eleanor was... special." She hesitated. "She kept to herself, especially lately. People in town had their opinions."

My brow furrowed. "What opinions?"

Mrs. Graham waved a hand dismissively, though her eyes stayed cautious.

"Small towns love gossip, dear. Best to ignore it. Let Eleanor rest

peacefully."

Something unspoken hung in the air, a quiet warning. Before I could ask more, Mrs. Graham stepped back. "I should get going. If you need anything, just knock."

The door clicked shut behind her, and silence returned. I picked up the diary. The leather cover was warm under my fingers.

Flipping through it, I found pages of Eleanor's neat handwriting notes, thoughts, and observations. Some mundane. Some... cryptic. One page caught my eye. The handwriting was rushed and uneven:

"Lila Carver... The trees whisper, and no one listens. They bury secrets deep, but I can't forget. I owe it to her."

I stared at the name. Lila Carver. It rang faintly familiar, an echo of whispered stories from my childhood, half-heard and half-believed.

Outside, the sun dipped low, casting long amber shadows. Inside, those shadows danced across the furniture like quiet ghosts. Eleanor's death had been ruled a heart attack, but something didn't feel right.

I set the diary back down. Not tonight. I needed rest.

Upstairs, Eleanor's guest room felt unchanged. Fresh sheets. Lavender sachets were tucked beneath the pillows. I slipped beneath the covers and tried to sleep. But the silence in Rosehill wasn't peaceful. It was watchful.

Eventually, exhaustion pulled me into uneasy dreams of whispers, of shadowy trees, and a girl named Lila, forever just out of reach.

 Morning sunlight streamed through the curtains. Disoriented, I sat up as the memories of yesterday returned with sharp clarity. Eleanor. The diary. Lila.

Then came the clink of porcelain. Footsteps downstairs. I grabbed a robe and crept down, heart thudding. In the kitchen stood a young man, about my age, neatly dressed with glasses and a shy smile. He looked up, startled. "Oh, sorry! Mrs. Graham gave me a key. I'm Sam Delaney, the librarian."

He motioned to a tray of pastries and coffee. "Thought you might need breakfast after the drive."

I relaxed slightly. "Thanks, Sam. That's kind of you."

He smiled. "Eleanor spoke of you. Proud but always a little sad."

"Sad?" I asked, stepping closer. He nodded. "She missed you. And... she seemed troubled. Lately,

especially."

"Why?"

"She never said. But she spent a lot of time researching Rosehill's past. One event, in particular."

"Lila Carver?"

Sam's eyes widened. "You found her diary, didn't you?"

I nodded, picking up a cup of coffee. "Hard to ignore cryptic clues and strange warnings."

Sam grew serious. "Rosehill doesn't like its past dug up, Maya. Eleanor asked questions people didn't want to answer."

I took a steadying breath. "And now I'm asking them."

He met my gaze with quiet respect. "Then be careful. The past doesn't always stay buried."

His words lingered after he left, their weight settling deep in my chest. Neighbors peeked from behind curtains. Watching. Waiting.

Rosehill hadn't changed, but I had. And I wasn't leaving until I uncovered the truth, no matter how deep or dark it was.

Chapter 2 The Inheritance

The morning sunlight softened Rosehill's edges, painting the quiet town in gentle hues. Still, the beauty felt hollow—a thin veneer barely concealing something deeper, darker. I stood on the porch, mug of coffee in hand, letting the warmth seep into my chilled fingers as I surveyed my inheritance. The house was beautiful—imposing, even—but it felt heavy with Eleanor's presence, her secrets woven into every faded floorboard.

A stack of legal documents from Eleanor's lawyer lay untouched on the kitchen table, stark and clinical against the rustic charm of the house. I sighed deeply, set the mug down, and forced myself to face reality. This wasn't just a nostalgic visit. Eleanor had left me everything: the sprawling house, her modest savings, and the whispered suspicions that lingered in her wake.

With a reluctant hand, I flipped through the documents—property deeds, financial accounts, and a brief handwritten letter from Eleanor, hastily penned. Her usually precise handwriting was shaky, uneven:

My dearest Maya, I know you & l make sense of this where I couldn't. Be careful who you trust. Rosehill's roots go deeper than you think. Love, Eleanor. A chill crept down my spine. The note held more weight than its brief words suggested. "Be careful who you trust." A vague warning, but in a town where every gaze felt laced with judgment, it felt sharp and deliberate.

I dressed quickly, urgency building in my chest. There were practical matters to handle—bank visits, groceries, utilities—but more importantly, I needed answers. About Eleanor. About Lila Carver. About a town that wore its charm like a mask.

Outside, the street was deceptively quiet. As I walked toward the town center, I felt eyes on me—watching from behind curtains and narrow doorways. Mrs. Graham offered a hesitant wave from her garden, her expression cautious, as though bracing for questions she didn't want to answer. The town square remained unchanged: small boutiques, an old-fashioned diner with vinyl

booths, and the stone-faced library standing solid and familiar. But underneath the nostalgia, something was off. Conversations stilled as I passed, voices dipping into uneasy murmurs.

"Miss Carter," someone called softly. I turned to see Detective Reynolds—retired but still commanding—standing near the bakery. His grizzled features held a quiet intensity.

"Detective," I greeted, wary. I remembered his name from news clippings tied to Lila Carver's case.

He stepped closer. "I hear you're staying. Eleanor's place is quite the inheritance."

"It is," I replied, cautious. "Though it seems to come with strings attached."

His gaze sharpened. "Rosehill always has strings, Maya. Your aunt knew that better than anyone. She'd have told you to leave—quickly."

I squared my shoulders. "Eleanor also wanted me to find something. Didn't she?"

He hesitated, clearly weighing his words. "She tried. But sometimes it's better to let old secrets lie."

"Better for whom?" I asked, irritation flaring.

He looked away. "Just be careful. Eleanor stirred things up. People here have long memories.

Not everyone wants the truth."

He tipped his hat slightly and walked away, leaving a silence that felt anything but peaceful.

The library was an oasis of calm—bright and orderly. Sam sat at the front desk, flipping through paperwork. He glanced up when the bell chimed.

"Maya. Back already?" he asked, setting his pen aside.

"Eleanor left me everything," I said softly. "The house. Her things… even her questions."

His expression darkened. "Have you decided what to do next?"

"I want to dig deeper," I said. "But I need help. Eleanor trusted you, didn't she?"

Sam nodded. "She did. She practically lived in the archives. Spent hours buried in old newspapers and records. She was chasing something specific."

"Lila Carver?"

Sam sighed and took off his glasses. "Yes. Lila disappeared before I was born, but her story shadows this town. People avoid talking about her—like pretending she never existed will make it true."

"Why?" I pressed. "What's so terrible that everyone would rather forget?"

"Influential families," he said quietly. "Especially the Hawthornes. Their name carries weight here. Eleanor believed they were hiding something."

"Then why didn't she go to the police?"

"She tried," he said sadly. "But evidence vanished. Reports were lost. Eventually, people just called her paranoid."

Anger stirred in my chest. "So she died being called crazy—for telling the truth?"

"Maybe," Sam said gently. "But you're here now. She must have believed you could finish what she started."

I nodded, my resolve hardening. "Then let's begin where she left off. Where's everything she was researching?"

Sam rose from his chair. "Follow me. But understand—once we start, there's no turning back." "I'm ready," I said, following him deeper into the library, into the dim archives where the air smelled of dust and forgotten stories.

As we walked, the shadows of Rosehill seemed to close in, heavier than ever. Eleanor's inheritance wasn't just a house or a bank account—it was a mystery. One steeped in silence, fear, and danger. And now, it was mine.

Chapter 3 The Locked Room

Days blurred together as I settled deeper into the rhythm of Rosehill, the town's charming façade still managing to conceal its secrets. Yet my mind clung to Eleanor's diary—her cryptic, urgent words calling out for answers from beyond the grave. One restless afternoon, determined to find something—anything—I decided to thoroughly explore the house. Eleanor had to have left more clues. I moved through rooms familiar from childhood—filled with antique furniture, portraits whose eyes seemed to follow me, shelves of books thick with dust.

Each space stirred memories, but offered little else. At the end of the upstairs hallway, I paused in front of the locked room. Eleanor had always kept it closed—off-limits. Even as a child, I'd felt a curious pull toward whatever lay behind that door.

I touched the ornate handle, feeling the weight of years and secrets. The lock was solid, its brass fittings cool beneath my fingers. No key had surfaced among Eleanor's things.

Frustration bubbled inside me. Without thinking, I hurried downstairs, found a toolbox in the pantry, grabbed a screwdriver, and returned—determined. Carefully, methodically, I began dismantling the lock. It resisted at first, the metal grinding in protest, but finally gave way with a reluctant click.

Heart pounding, I eased the door open. Sunlight filtered through heavy curtains, illuminating swirling dust motes in the still air. The room smelled stale, sealed off from fresh air for years. It was simply furnished: a single bed covered with an embroidered quilt, an old wooden desk, bookshelves lined with faded volumes, and a

worn armchair tucked into the corner.

Despite its quiet simplicity, the room thrummed with a strange intensity, as if every object carried hidden meaning.

I was immediately drawn to the desk. It was meticulously arranged—an antique brass lamp, a stack of neatly folded stationery, and at the center, another leather-bound diary identical to the one downstairs. My pulse surged.

I picked it up, its familiar weight grounding me. Cautiously—almost reverently—I opened it. Eleanor's handwriting spilled across the pages, becoming increasingly erratic with each passing date. It was a mirror of her unraveling mind.

I sank into the armchair, compelled to read.

April 14: Rosehill's silence is deafening. Everyone pretends ignorance, but their eyes betray knowledge. They know what happened to Lila, yet silence binds them tighter than fear.

June 22: Detective Reynolds warned me today. Said I should leave it alone. He meant well, but he doesn't understand. I can't stop. Lila deserves justice.

My breath quickened, the words gripping me like a vice. I flipped ahead, each entry more urgent, more panicked.

July 19: The shadows lengthen. Strange cars idle outside my house at night. Sam insists it's nothing, but I feel their eyes. They want me to stop digging.

August 3: They're watching constantly now. Notes left on my doorstep, whispered threats in grocery aisles. The Hawthornes have reach everywhere. They know I'm close.

My heart pounded. Was Eleanor slipping into paranoia—or had she uncovered something real?

I turned to the entries near the end, just before her death.

October 5: Sam believes me. At least I have an ally. He found newspaper clippings—reports about Lila's disappearance. Someone tried erasing her existence, but left clues behind.

November 12: I think they're planning something. Strange cars tail me everywhere. Shadows linger constantly. But I won't stop.

The final entry, dated two days before Eleanor died, sent ice down my spine:

November 16: If anyone finds this, know my death wasn't accidental. The truth is in the bank—locked in a safety deposit box. Trust no one, Maya. Especially not those who smile

brightest. I closed the diary slowly, Eleanor's words weighing heavy on my chest. She'd known she was in danger. This wasn't just fear—it was foresight. A warning.

A sudden knock echoed from downstairs, making me jump. I hastily tucked the diary beneath a pile of papers and steadied myself before heading down.

I opened the front door cautiously. Detective Reynolds stood there, his expression grave.

"Maya," he said, his voice heavy with something between concern and resignation. "We need to

talk."

Eleanor's warning rang in my ears: Trust no one.

"Come in," I said guardedly, stepping aside.

He entered, glancing around with visible unease. "You opened the locked room, didn't you?"

My eyes narrowed. "How could you possibly know that?"

He hesitated. "Because Eleanor told me. She believed that room was the key to everything."

Suspicion coiled in my gut. "And yet you told her to stop digging."

"To protect her," Reynolds said, frustration slipping into his voice. "You don't understand how dangerous this can get."

"Then explain it," I pressed. "What was Eleanor trying to uncover?"

He sighed deeply, shoulders sagging. "Lila Carver disappeared decades ago, but not without reason. Some people still living in this town benefit from keeping it unresolved."

"The Hawthornes?" I asked pointedly. He flinched slightly, eyes flicking to the window. "Exactly. Eleanor believed she found something solid—proof hidden in a bank safety deposit box. She never got to retrieve it."

"Did you try?" I asked.

"Yes," he admitted grimly. "But the box requires Eleanor's key—and her personal code. I found

neither."

"I will," I said with growing resolve. "Eleanor wouldn't leave things unfinished."

His expression softened slightly. "Just be careful, Maya. You're treading in deep waters."

"Dangerous or not, I owe this to Eleanor."

He nodded once, his gaze filled with something like admiration—and fear. "This town watches. It listens. Be careful who you trust."

When he left, silence crept back in. I climbed the stairs and retrieved the diary, holding it like a sacred artifact. Eleanor's voice echoed in my head: Trust no one.

Rosehill's charm had fully shattered, revealing rot beneath the surface. Every smile felt suspicious. Every neighbor is a possible threat.

My inheritance wasn't just Eleanor's house—it was her unfinished quest. A mystery steeped in danger. A life cut short.

I stood at the window, staring at the street below. Curtains shifted. Eyes watched. Eleanor had died searching for answers. Now, her secrets were mine to uncover—no matter the

cost. The locked room had given up its first crucial secret—but the hardest truths lay buried deeper, waiting ominously in shadows.

Chapter 4 The Diary's Clue

I didn't sleep that night.

Even after Detective Reynolds left and the house settled into its creaking nighttime hush, the echo of Eleanor's diary entries kept repeating in my head. Lila Carver. Safety deposit box. Trust no one. Especially those who smile brightest.

I had no idea who Lila Carver really was—not beyond the name Eleanor scribbled like a mantra in nearly every journal entry. And while Reynolds confirmed she'd gone missing decades ago, the real story remained locked away, buried beneath fear and silence. That kind of mystery doesn't linger this long without purpose. Or protection.

At dawn, I sat in the kitchen cradling a mug of lukewarm tea. The light over the sink flickered as the morning sun crept across the counters. Eleanor had been trying to show me something. And now it was my job to find it.

I returned to the locked room, Eleanor's final refuge. Dust still lingered in the air like a presence, a veil between past and present. I opened the diary again, this time with a yellow legal pad at my side. If I was going to unravel this mystery, I had to treat it like what it was: an investigation.

Page by page, I documented patterns in Eleanor's notes. Names that recurred: Lila Carver, the Hawthornes, Sam, Reynolds. Places too—Rosehill Library, Greenhill Campground, Westwood Cemetery.

It wasn't until I reached the August entries that something clicked.

"August 11: The tree again. The same twisted trunk in every memory. Lila stood beneath it in that photo, laughing. The photo's gone now, but I remember the symbol carved into the bark: a crescent and a cross. They all said it was a ghost story, but it wasn't. It was the last place she was seen."

The tree. A symbol. A location. It wasn't much, but it was something.

I flipped back through the diary, searching for any other mention of the tree. In a June entry, Eleanor described walking through the woods near Greenhill Campground and finding it again—"just as broken and bent as I remember."

So I had a place. A trailhead.

I packed a backpack—flashlight, water bottle, granola bars, gloves—and tucked Eleanor's diary inside. The entry made it sound like the tree marked something. A memory. A moment frozen in time.

The drive to Greenhill Campground took twenty minutes. The road curved through thickets of dense pine, the canopy above weaving sunlight into sharp golden shards. The campground had clearly seen better days: weathered picnic tables, a rusted water pump, and an unmanned ranger shack covered in flyers warning hikers about ticks and trail erosion.

I parked on the outskirts, grabbed my pack, and followed the trail eastward as Eleanor had once described. The air was heavy with the scent of damp leaves and moss. Birds flitted overhead, chirping like indifferent guardians of these woods. The further I walked, the quieter it became—until even the chirping stopped.

It took over an hour of hiking to find the tree.

It stood just off the path, a gnarled oak so bent it looked like it was bowing to the earth. The bark was cracked, the roots coiled like serpents beneath the dirt. And on the northern side, just where Eleanor had said—it was there.

A crescent moon and cross, crudely carved. Old but distinct. It didn't belong in the woods. It didn't belong anywhere.

I knelt beside the trunk and touched the bark. It felt dry and cold, like bone. I circled the tree slowly, looking for anything that could explain why Eleanor had marked this so clearly in her diary.

At the base of the trunk, beneath a tangle of ivy, I found it: a rusted tin box, wedged between root and earth.

My fingers trembled as I pried it free. The lid gave with a metallic groan, revealing yellowed newspaper clippings, a faded photograph, and a letter folded into quarters. I sat cross-legged in the dirt, heart pounding.

The photograph came first. A black-and-white shot of two girls—one unmistakably Eleanor, the other younger, with wild curls and a mischievous smile. Lila. It had to be. They stood beneath this very tree.

The newspaper clipping was dated June 14, 1987. The headline read: "Teen Girl Disappears from Rosehill Campground."

Lila Carver, age 16, last seen near Greenhill Campground. Local authorities cite lack of evidence, no witnesses. Investigation ongoing.

The article had a photograph of Lila, grainy and poorly lit, but it was clearly the same girl from Eleanor's photo.

The letter was addressed to Eleanor. The handwriting was shaky.

Eleanor, I'm sorry I ran. I didn't know what else to do. I was scared—he said he'd kill me if I told anyone. But I couldn't disappear completely. Not without saying goodbye. You were the only one who listened. Thank you for believing me.

—Lila

I reread it twice. Then a third time. If Lila had written this, then she hadn't vanished like everyone believed. She ran. But from who?

The letter didn't name him. But Eleanor clearly believed the answer lay with the Hawthornes.

As I packed the items back into the tin, footsteps crunched on the trail behind me. I froze.

"Maya?" a voice called—familiar but cautious.

Sam.

Relieved, I stepped into view. He blinked, startled.

"What are you doing all the way out here?"

"Following Eleanor's clues," I said, holding up the diary. "And finding Lila's voice. She didn't just disappear, Sam. She ran. Someone threatened her."

Sam crouched beside the tree, inspecting the carving. "The crescent and cross. I've seen that before. There's graffiti with that symbol behind the old church. I thought it was kids playing around."

"Maybe it's more than that," I said. "Maybe it's a mark. A sign of something darker."

He stood up, brushing dirt from his knees. "This just got more complicated. If Lila left that letter... then the official story is a lie."

I nodded. "And someone made sure it stayed that way."

We hiked back in silence, our thoughts heavier than the forest shadows. Back at the car, I handed Sam the photograph.

"We need to find out who else knew her. And why she was so afraid."

He looked up. "There's one person who might talk. Bartender at the Maplewood Inn. He's been here since the '80s. If anyone remembers Lila, it's him."

We agreed to go the next night.

As I drove back toward Eleanor's house, I looked in the rearview mirror. A dark SUV followed me at a distance for several miles before turning off.

Coincidence? Maybe. But I was starting to believe that word didn't exist in Rosehill.

Back at the house, I laid the photo and the letter on the kitchen table. The girls in the picture were happy once. Innocent. Whatever happened in the woods took that away. Not just from Lila —but from Eleanor too.

Now it had become my burden.

I opened the diary to the August 11 entry again and underlined Eleanor's words: *They all said it was a ghost story, but it wasn't.*

No. It wasn't.

It was the beginning of the truth. And the end of someone's silence.

Chapter 5 Town of Shadows

The next morning, Rosehill was cloaked in fog, a thick mist curling through the streets like a restless spirit. It softened the edges of the town, turning familiar houses into ghostly silhouettes and muffling the sound of distant cars. Even the birds were quiet.

I pulled my jacket tighter and stepped out into the cool air, the photograph of Eleanor and Lila folded in my pocket. I wasn't planning to show it around just yet—but I wanted it close, a talisman reminding me why I was here.

As I walked through the town square, I noticed something peculiar. Conversations paused when I approached. Eyes followed me— some curious, others cautious. I passed the diner and caught sight of Mrs. Graham through the window, sipping coffee with two other women. They didn't wave. They turned their heads as if I were a sudden chill in the air.

The sense of isolation was growing heavier with every step.

I ducked into the Rosehill Pharmacy, a small, dimly lit shop that smelled of antiseptic and floor polish. An older man with wire-rimmed glasses stood behind the counter, flipping through a worn ledger.

"Morning," I offered.

He looked up, startled. "Ah. Morning. Can I help you?"

"I was wondering if you remembered a girl named Lila Carver," I asked, keeping my tone light. "She went missing in the '80s."

His expression shuttered. "That was a long time ago."

"I know. My aunt, Eleanor Carter, was looking into it before she died. I'm just... curious."

The man's fingers tightened around his pen. "Eleanor asked a lot of questions too. Made people uncomfortable."

"Why?" I asked.

"She had a habit of turning over stones best left untouched."

He turned back to his ledger without another word.

Outside, the fog had thickened. The town felt like it was closing in.

Next, I stopped by the hardware store, hoping for a friendlier face. The bell jingled overhead, and a woman in her fifties looked up from the register. Her eyes widened slightly when she saw me.

"You're Eleanor's niece," she said.

"I am. Maya Carter."

She nodded slowly, setting down the receipt she was folding. "I'm Janet. I remember you from summers, when you were small. Used to buy penny candy from my husband."

I smiled, encouraged. "I'm actually looking into some things Eleanor left behind. She was... investigating something before she died."

Janet's smile faded. "Yes. Lila."

I blinked. "So you do remember her."

She hesitated, visibly torn. "We were in the same graduating class. Quiet girl. Pretty. Got along with most people, but she had secrets. Secrets tend to fester in places like this."

"What happened to her?"

"I don't know," Janet said slowly. "No one does. Or maybe they do, but won't say. When she vanished, it was like the town held its breath and never let it out again."

"That's how Eleanor made it sound. Like there was a blanket of silence over everything."

"She tried to pull it off." Janet's eyes darkened. "And people didn't like that. Thought she was unstable. Paranoid. She started writing letters, posting flyers about corruption and conspiracies. Most of them were torn down the same day."

"But was she wrong?"

Janet gave a long, tired sigh. "Maybe not. But around here, truth isn't always welcome. Especially when it rattles the wrong cages."

I thanked her and left, heart heavy with a strange combination of frustration and clarity. Eleanor hadn't been paranoid—at least, not without reason. She'd known something rotten lurked under the town's manicured lawns and pristine sidewalks.

I wandered aimlessly until I found myself back in front of the church. It was empty, the heavy doors ajar. Inside, the air was cool and still. The sanctuary was lined with pews and stained-glass windows depicting saints with solemn eyes.

As I walked down the aisle, I noticed faint markings on the wall near the back—small symbols scratched into the plaster. One of them, half-hidden behind a hymn board, caught my eye: a crescent and cross.

The same as on the tree.

My breath caught.

"Looking for something?"

The voice came from the back pew. An elderly woman sat there, draped in a gray shawl, her hands folded neatly in her lap.

"Just... visiting," I replied.

She smiled faintly. "You're Eleanor's girl."

I nodded. "She was my aunt."

"She came here often. Sat in that very pew. Prayed for justice. Or maybe for peace. Maybe both."

"Did you know her well?"

"Well enough," the woman said. "She was brave. Too brave for a town like this."

"What do you mean?"

"She asked questions. Pushed people. She believed in things no one else dared believe in. That makes you dangerous around here."

I sat across from her, the symbol burning in my mind. "What does the crescent and cross mean?"

The woman tilted her head. "A warning. A place marked by tragedy. The children made up stories about it. But the truth is always harder to swallow than fiction."

"And what's the truth?" I asked.

She looked past me, eyes distant. "It's buried. Beneath silence. Beneath fear. And fear is what keeps Rosehill safe—for some."

She stood slowly, her shawl falling like a veil around her shoulders. "Be careful, Maya. People here wear masks that have been passed down for generations."

She walked away, leaving me alone with the pews and the past.

When I returned to Eleanor's house, I felt the weight of the town pressing against the windows. Rosehill wasn't just evasive. It was actively resisting.

Eleanor had seen that. She'd tried to pull back the curtain. And they'd called her paranoid for it.

Now I was following in her footsteps—and I was starting to understand just how dangerous that path really was.

Chapter 6 A Message From the Past

It was nearing dusk when I finally stopped walking.

After the church visit and my brief, uneasy conversations around town, I'd wandered without direction, trying to shake the weight of the day. I told myself I was clearing my head, but deep down I knew the truth: I was avoiding going home. Avoiding the silence, the shadows in Eleanor's house, and the echo of her desperate scribbles.

Instead, I found myself on the edge of the historic district— Rosehill's oldest neighborhood. The houses here were timeworn and proud, each one stooped slightly with age, as though bowed under the pressure of decades of secrets.

I stopped in front of one in particular: a weather-beaten yellow cottage tucked behind a wild garden of untrimmed hedges and wilting roses. I remembered it vaguely from childhood walks with Eleanor, but I couldn't place who lived there.

Then the front door creaked open.

"Thought you might show up here."

The voice was rasped and low, like paper dragged across wood. An old woman stood in the doorway, wrapped in a crocheted shawl, her silver hair braided down her back. Her gaze was direct, unblinking.

"I'm sorry, do I—"

"Your aunt brought you by once. You were small then. Too young to understand the kind of place this is."

I stepped closer. "You knew Eleanor?"

She nodded. "We weren't friends. But we had...common concerns."

I paused. "Concerns like Lila Carver?"

Her expression didn't change, but the pause in her breathing was enough. "Come in. Before someone sees you here."

Inside, the house smelled of mint tea and musty paper. Dozens of old photographs lined the mantle, and a table near the window was stacked with newspaper clippings, some yellowed with age. I recognized a few headlines instantly: Lila's disappearance, Eleanor's obituary, and several articles about the Hawthornes and their political reach.

"You've been keeping records," I said softly.

"Someone had to." The woman gestured for me to sit. "My name's Virginia. I used to teach at Rosehill High. Lila was one of mine."

I blinked. "You were her teacher?"

"She was quiet but smart. Kept to herself, but there was a sadness to her. That kind of sadness doesn't come from nowhere."

I handed her the photo I'd found beneath the tree. She took it without surprise.

"She gave this to Eleanor," I said. "Before she ran. Or disappeared. Or was taken."

Virginia's hand trembled slightly as she passed the photo back. "She was scared. Came to me a week before she vanished. Said she couldn't stay here. Said someone hurt her. Someone powerful. But she wouldn't name names."

"Do you think it was one of the Hawthornes?"

"I know it was," she whispered. "But knowing and proving are two different things."

"Did you tell anyone?"

"I told the police. They dismissed me. Told me not to stir up drama. Said girls like Lila run off all the time."

I felt my stomach churn. "And you never heard from her again?"

Virginia gave me a long, haunted look. "Not directly. But Eleanor came by not long after. Said she'd gotten a letter. Said Lila trusted her."

"She did. I found the letter. She thanked Eleanor for believing her."

Virginia nodded. "Your aunt was stubborn. Brave. Foolish too. Thought truth alone could shake this town's foundation."

"And now I'm doing the same," I said.

Virginia stood slowly, walking over to the window and pulling the curtain back just an inch. "Then you should know what you're walking into. This place doesn't just hide its shadows—it feeds on them. It thrives on silence."

I stood too, the words catching in my throat. "Are you telling me to stop?"

She didn't turn. "I'm telling you this town never forgets. And it never forgives. You're stirring waters that want to stay still. You might not like what floats to the surface."

I stepped toward the door, unsettled. "So what should I do? Pretend none of this happened? Let Lila vanish into history?"

Virginia turned then, eyes fierce. "No. But be smarter than Eleanor. She let her rage cloud her caution. Don't let yours blind you."

Outside, night had fallen. The fog had returned, thick and clinging. As I walked back toward the house, I couldn't help but glance over my shoulder. The shadows of Rosehill stretched longer now, darker than before.

A message from the past had been delivered.

It hadn't come with answers.

But it had come with a warning.

Chapter 7: Library Files

The library felt different today.

It wasn't the lighting or the temperature, or even the faint smell of lemon cleaner and old paper that always clung to the walls—it was the weight. The knowledge that Eleanor had sat here, digging through records, chasing ghosts, only to end up dead. The knowledge that I might be next if I didn't figure out what she had uncovered.

Sam met me at the front desk, holding two travel mugs of coffee and a manila folder so thick it looked like it might burst.

"Thought you'd need fuel," he said, handing me one of the cups.

"Librarian and barista," I teased, but my voice lacked levity.

He gave me a knowing look. "You didn't sleep either."

"Not a wink."

He motioned for me to follow. "I pulled all the records Eleanor accessed in the last three months. Some of it's from the town archives, some from our private records. She had a pattern—I think you'll see it."

We descended into the lower level of the library, the oldest part of the building. The air was cooler here, and the silence deeper, almost reverent. It smelled like secrets.

He led me to a long, narrow room lined with metal cabinets and tall bookshelves. A table had already been cleared for us, scattered with town ledgers, microfilm reels, yellowed newspaper clippings, and a few yearbooks.

"This is where she spent most of her time," Sam said. "Sometimes she was here until closing, scribbling in a notebook, mumbling to herself. I thought she was just... eccentric. Now I'm not so sure."

I pulled out Eleanor's diary from my bag and opened it to a page marked with a torn ribbon. "She wasn't mumbling. She was connecting dots. Look at this." I read aloud from the entry dated August 21st:

"Met with Sam. Found mention of a cleanup crew at Greenhill Campground a week before Lila vanished. Councilman Graham Hawthorne led it. Coincidence? No. Feels staged. Feels like a smokescreen."

Sam's face tightened. "She never told me she suspected Graham."

"She probably didn't want to scare you off." I scanned the documents on the table. "Do you have the newspaper from that week?"

Sam handed me a brittle page folded neatly in a plastic sleeve. The headline read:

TOWN VOLUNTEERS SCHEDULED TO CLEAN GREENHILL CAMPGROUND – June 6, 1987
A community effort led by Councilman Graham Hawthorne aims to restore Greenhill Campground before summer. Cleanup to include forested trail system. Volunteers welcome.

I looked up. "If Lila disappeared on June 14, this was exactly one week before."

"Eleanor marked it too," Sam said, flipping to another folder. "She underlined the word 'forested.' That's the area where you found the photo and the letter, right?"

"Yeah." I frowned. "Do you think they used the cleanup as cover? Or to bury something?"

"Maybe both," he said grimly.

We sifted through more articles. One was a missing person bulletin featuring Lila's school photo, her smile small and tentative.

Another was an opinion column, dated a month later, criticizing the police department's failure to find leads.

Sam slid a photo toward me. "This one shook me. Found it deep in the archives. Taken at a summer block party in 1986."

I studied the image. A group of teenagers clustered together around a barbecue. Lila stood off to the side, eyes downcast. Behind her was a young man, mid-twenties, tall, wearing sunglasses.

"Who is that?" I asked.

"Name's James Hawthorne. Graham's nephew. Taught at Rosehill High for a year before he abruptly resigned. Quiet guy. No one talks about him much."

I shivered. "Maybe because they were told not to."

Sam leaned in. "Eleanor believed he was the one Lila was running from."

I felt the weight of that name. Hawthorne. It kept coming up like a stain that wouldn't wash out.

"Anything on police records?" I asked.

He handed me a thin file. "Reynolds filed a report on Lila's case when he was still active duty. He tried, but every lead vanished—literally. Witness statements removed, evidence never catalogued. Eleanor annotated the margins: 'Suppression?'"

"Or a cover-up," I muttered. "How high did this go?"

Sam looked around, voice dropping. "Eleanor believed the Hawthornes controlled not just the police, but the church, the council, even some of the local press. She thought Rosehill was a kingdom—and they were its monarchy."

"And Lila?" I asked. "Just collateral?"

He hesitated, then opened another folder and pulled out a torn page from a student essay.

"Eleanor found this in a box marked 'Rosehill High – 1987 Seniors.' It's unsigned. But it talks about a secret relationship, fear, and an 'accident that wasn't.'" He pushed it toward me.

I read aloud:

"I know what happened that night. She didn't fall. She didn't run. It was planned. He said no one would ever find her. That she'd vanish like a ghost. I wanted to scream. But I didn't. I watched. And I let it happen."

I looked up. "This is a confession."

Sam nodded. "Or a witness afraid to name names. Either way, it's chilling."

I sat back in my chair, overwhelmed. "Eleanor must have found all this and realized she wasn't dealing with folklore. This wasn't just a small-town mystery. It was a conspiracy."

"She wasn't crazy," Sam said quietly. "She was just too loud about it."

We sat in silence, the hum of the old library lights buzzing overhead. Then Sam cleared his throat.

"I think it's time we visit Megan Ellis. She was Lila's closest friend. If anyone knows more—it's her."

"You trust her?" I asked.

"I don't trust anyone," he said. "But I think she might be tired of staying silent."

We packed the documents into a satchel, along with copies of the photos and articles. Sam locked up the archives, and we exited through the back door, unnoticed.

Outside, the sky had darkened, and a cold wind whipped through the trees.

"You sure about this?" Sam asked as we approached his car.

"No," I admitted. "But I'm not stopping."

He nodded and opened the passenger door. "Then let's see what Megan remembers. Before someone else decides to make us forget."

Chapter 8 Breaking Into the Past

Megan Ellis's antique shop sat at the far end of Birch Street, nestled between an old tailor and a boarded-up bakery. Its front window was cluttered with cracked porcelain dolls, faded postcards, and dusty silverware—more a shrine to forgotten things than a place of business.

"I called ahead," Sam said as we stepped inside. "Told her we wanted to talk about Eleanor."

A bell jingled above the door, and the scent of cedar and old linen wrapped around us like a curtain. From behind a glass case filled with vintage brooches, a woman in her late forties looked up. Her auburn hair was streaked with gray, pulled into a loose bun, and her eyes—narrow, appraising—landed on me.

"You must be Maya," she said.

"I am."

"I was sorry to hear about Eleanor," Megan said, rounding the case. "She had her demons, but she meant well."

"She wasn't wrong, though, was she?" I asked. "About Lila?"

Something shifted behind Megan's eyes. A wall. A memory.

"Come to the back," she said quietly.

We followed her through a bead curtain into a smaller room cluttered with trunks and picture frames. She pulled down a shade over the window and motioned for us to sit.

"You're the first person to ask me about Lila in almost twenty years," she said. "Most folks have chosen to forget."

"I can't afford to forget," I said. "Neither could Eleanor."

Megan looked at Sam. "You were always a sweet kid. I'm guessing you didn't drag her into this lightly."

He gave a small shrug. "She's not exactly the dragging type."

Megan's gaze returned to me. "Lila was my best friend. Like a sister. She confided in me more than anyone. She told me about... James."

"James Hawthorne?" I asked, heart thudding.

"Yes. He was older, charming, dangerous. At first, I thought it was a silly crush, but then she stopped coming to school some mornings. Started hiding bruises under sweaters. I asked her about them. She made excuses."

"And then she disappeared," I said.

Megan nodded. "I blamed myself. I still do. A week before she vanished, she asked me if I believed someone could fake their own disappearance."

"She was planning it?" Sam asked.

"She wanted out. But she was scared. Said James had friends everywhere—police, council, even church elders. Said if she tried to leave, he'd make sure no one ever found her."

"Did she say why he was so possessive?" I asked.

Megan hesitated. "She thought she was pregnant."

The words landed like a blow. Sam leaned back, eyes wide.

"And she told Eleanor?" I pressed.

"She wrote her a letter," Megan said. "I never saw it, but Eleanor came to me a week after Lila disappeared. Told me she'd do everything she could to find her."

"She did," I said. "She kept digging until the day she died."

Megan reached under the table and pulled out a faded shoebox. Inside were more photos of Lila—at school dances, birthday parties, the two of them sitting on swings. Beneath the photos was a single cassette tape.

"I found this in Lila's locker after she disappeared. I never told anyone. I couldn't risk it. But you should hear it."

She handed me a dusty cassette player and pressed play.

A soft hiss filled the room, then a trembling voice.

"If anyone finds this... I'm sorry. I didn't want it to end like this. I'm scared. He says I belong to him. That if I leave, he'll make me disappear like the others. I don't know who to trust. But if you're hearing this, it means I didn't make it. Tell Eleanor... thank you."

The tape clicked off.

I sat in stunned silence, breath caught in my throat. The fear in Lila's voice wasn't just palpable—it was paralyzing.

"She knew," I whispered. "She knew he would kill her."

Megan looked down. "And we all let it happen."

I stared at the tape in my hands. "This is enough to reopen the case."

Megan's expression hardened. "Do you really believe that? You think the Hawthornes haven't buried worse? You think this tape won't 'accidentally' disappear the moment you hand it over?"

"She's right," Sam said. "We need something concrete. Something public. Something they can't erase."

I glanced at him. "The safety deposit box. Eleanor mentioned it in her final diary entry. Said it held the final truth."

Megan stood. "Then get to it before they do."

That night, we broke in.

Not into the bank itself—but into Eleanor's desk, the locked drawer I'd overlooked in my search.

We found it at the back, under a false panel: a slim brass key and a folded slip of paper with a six-digit code.

"Her handwriting," I said. "She wanted me to find this."

Sam exhaled. "Then tomorrow, we go to the bank."

"I'll go," I said. "Alone. If something happens... you stay out of it."

"Maya—"

"No." I looked him in the eye. "This is my family. My burden."

Sam nodded, reluctant but understanding. "Then at least let me walk you there."

The bank in Rosehill was a brick-and-glass relic from the '70s, its lobby lined with potted ficus trees and framed photos of board members. I walked in just after opening, the key tucked in my palm.

"I'd like to access a safety deposit box," I told the teller.

She smiled politely, took my ID, then led me down a carpeted corridor. The vault smelled like old steel and dry paper. She gestured to box 117 and left me alone.

My hands trembled as I inserted the key and turned.

Inside was a single envelope marked *In case they silence me.*

I opened it slowly.

Inside were photographs—Eleanor and Lila together, smiling under the twisted tree. A second photo of a hospital form, confirming Lila's pregnancy. And at the bottom, a typed confession signed only *J.H.*

"I never meant to hurt her. But I couldn't let her go. She was carrying my child. I told my uncle we had a problem. He said he'd make it go away. I didn't know how far he would go. By the time I tried to stop it, it was done."

I pressed the envelope to my chest, shaking.

This was it. The truth Eleanor had died to preserve.

I exited the vault and walked into the morning light of Rosehill.

I wasn't running anymore. And I wasn't afraid.

But someone else should be.

Chapter 9 Car Trouble

The next morning brought a strange silence to Rosehill. Not the usual small-town quiet, but something different—heavier. Watchful. Like the entire town was holding its breath, waiting for someone to make the wrong move.

I tucked Eleanor's key and the envelope back into my bag, careful not to crease the confession. The photographs, especially the one of the hospital form, felt like live wires in my possession—fragile but powerful.

I had the truth. Finally. Tangible, undeniable, damning truth.

Now I needed to figure out what to do with it.

Sam and I had agreed to meet that morning at the diner to talk about next steps. I locked the front door behind me and jogged down the porch steps, fishing for my keys as I approached my car.

That's when I saw it.

All four tires were slashed.

At first, I didn't believe it. I stood there staring, like maybe the morning light was playing tricks. But no—each tire was deflated, deep cuts visible along the sidewalls, as though someone had taken a knife to them methodically.

My hands trembled. This wasn't vandalism. This was a message.

I scanned the street. Nothing. No one. Every window was closed, every porch empty. I could feel them watching, though—behind curtains, behind silence. Rosehill didn't need to shout to intimidate. It whispered in tire rubber and broken glass.

I pulled out my phone and called Sam.

"What's wrong?" he asked, voice immediately alert.

"They got to my car," I said. "All four tires. Slashed."

Silence on the other end. Then: "Stay put. I'm coming to get you."

Ten minutes later, Sam's dusty sedan rolled up to the curb. He didn't speak at first, just stared at the damage as I climbed in.

"They're escalating," I said. "They know I have something."

Sam nodded grimly. "And they want to scare you into silence."

"It's not going to work," I said, but my voice shook. "It's just going to make me louder."

He pulled away from the curb. "Then let's figure out how to use what you have. Fast."

Back at the library, we laid the contents of the safety deposit envelope out on the archive table—each item placed like evidence in a trial.

The photos. The hospital form. The confession.

"They won't stay quiet if we go to the police," I said. "They'll bury it. Or say it's fake. Or blame Eleanor again."

Sam leaned over the confession. "This signature—J.H.—could be James Hawthorne, but it could also be a forgery. Without a verified match, it's still circumstantial."

"Then we get a match."

"And how do we do that?" he asked. "We're not detectives. We're barely functioning adults."

I smirked. "Speak for yourself."

But the question hung heavy. How could we prove the confession was legitimate?

Then I remembered something.

"The yearbooks," I said. "Didn't you say we had one from 1987?"

Sam pulled it from the shelf. We flipped to the faculty page. James Hawthorne—Science Department. Under his name, a teacher's signature—clean, fluid, the same looped 'J' and distinctive slant on the 'H.'

I pulled the confession over and laid the signatures side-by-side.

It was a match.

"Still not forensic," Sam said, "but it's enough to raise eyebrows."

"Then we raise them. With the right people."

We sat in silence, thinking.

"I have a friend," Sam said slowly. "Jenna. She's a reporter for a regional paper out of Harrisburg. Investigative, credible, and she hates corruption."

"Will she publish this?"

"She'll verify it. She'll run the story if it checks out. But we'll need to scan everything. Digitize the confession, the letter from Lila, the photos, everything."

I nodded. "Let's do it."

—

While Sam worked at the scanner, I stepped outside for air. The sun had risen higher now, burning through the fog. Still, something felt off.

My phone buzzed. A number I didn't recognize.

I hesitated, then answered.

"Miss Carter," a man's voice said. "You're stirring a lot of dust. I'd advise you to stop."

I froze. "Who is this?"

"Someone who doesn't want to see you get hurt. Eleanor didn't listen. Look where it got her."

My breath caught.

"You think threatening me is going to stop this?"

"It's not a threat," the voice said calmly. "It's a reminder. You're playing in the shadows. And the shadows play back."

The call ended.

I stared at the screen, pulse thudding in my ears. My stomach turned with equal parts fear and fury.

Back inside, I told Sam about the call. He stopped scanning and looked at me.

"They know we're moving forward."

"Then we're doing the right thing," I said. "Let them come."

That afternoon, we emailed Jenna everything. Scans, files, summaries of our findings, names. We used encrypted services and a VPN Sam had set up on his laptop.

She responded quickly.

Got the files. Reading now. Will verify before contact. Hold tight.

It was a small light. But in Rosehill, even a small light burned like a beacon.

By nightfall, we returned to Eleanor's house. Sam parked around back and helped me board up the garage. Just in case.

"I don't think they'll stop," I said, nailing the last plank. "Even if we publish."

"They won't," he agreed. "But we'll have exposed them. That's the start."

We sat on the porch in the dark, listening to the town around us creak and shift like it was alive.

Somewhere out there, James Hawthorne—or whoever was still protecting his legacy—was getting nervous.

I wanted them to be.

I wanted them to know that the silence was over.

Tomorrow, I would face whatever came. Because someone had slashed my tires thinking it would make me leave.

But I wasn't going anywhere.

Chapter 10 The Family Name

The next morning, I woke to find a manila envelope slipped under Eleanor's front door.

It wasn't marked. No return address. Just my name written in all caps across the front.

I stared at it for a long time before picking it up. Something about the weight—too light to be harmless, too heavy to ignore—made my hands tremble. Sam was still asleep on the couch, his laptop blinking softly beside him. I crept into the kitchen and opened the envelope under the light of Eleanor's old pendant lamp.

Inside were photographs.

Black and white. Grainy.

The first showed Eleanor and a young man—James Hawthorne—arguing in front of the church steps. Eleanor's face was red with fury; his, stony. Behind them, a crowd blurred in the background. On the back, a date was written: *August 3, 1987.*

The second photo showed Eleanor alone, holding a file, staring down a long hallway I didn't recognize.

The third was of me.

It was from yesterday—taken as I stood outside the library, phone pressed to my ear.

I dropped the photos onto the table, a chill crawling over my skin.

Whoever was watching Eleanor had turned their lens on me.

I woke Sam and showed him the photos. His jaw clenched, eyes scanning the one of me with dark understanding.

"We're running out of time," he said.

"No," I corrected. "They are."

—

We decided it was time to confront the Hawthornes directly.

The Hawthorne estate sat on the edge of Rosehill like a crown on a hill—four acres of stone walls, wrought iron, and manicured lies. It was a fortress, built not for beauty but for permanence. Wealth, old and inherited, had a way of rewriting the town's narrative. And the Hawthornes had been doing it for over a century.

Graham Hawthorne, the patriarch, was nearing 80 now, but still active on town council. His name appeared on plaques, the local school auditorium, even the new park. His nephew, James, had disappeared after Lila's vanishing, supposedly moved to Europe.

We parked a block away and approached on foot. The gate was closed, but the intercom beside it still buzzed to life when I pressed the button.

"Yes?" A woman's voice, clipped and cold.

"My name is Maya Carter. I'd like to speak to Councilman Hawthorne."

A pause. Then, "What about?"

"About Eleanor Carter. And Lila Carver."

Another pause. Longer. Then the gates buzzed open.

Sam shot me a look. "You sure about this?"

"No," I said. "But I'm going in."

We walked up the drive slowly. A gardener paused his trimming to watch us pass. A security camera above the door tilted slightly.

A woman in a gray suit answered. "Mr. Hawthorne will see you in the study. This way."

The house was as imposing inside as out—dark wood, oil portraits, old books, the smell of polish and power. She led us down a hall into a room lined with shelves and one massive window overlooking the backyard.

Graham Hawthorne sat in a leather chair, cane resting beside him. His posture was straight, his presence commanding despite the weight of age.

"I remember you," he said, eyes narrowed. "Eleanor's niece. The one who left and didn't come back until she was dead."

My fists clenched, but I kept my voice steady. "I came back to finish what she started."

He chuckled dryly. "She always had a flair for dramatics."

"She also had a file. On Lila. And on your nephew."

Graham's smile faded. "My nephew left town thirty years ago."

"No, he disappeared thirty years ago," I countered. "Right after Lila did."

"You're chasing ghosts, Miss Carter."

"Ghosts don't slash tires," I snapped. "They don't follow people or photograph them. But someone connected to your family is doing that."

Graham stood, slowly. "You're speaking in riddles. And you're wasting my time."

"I have his confession," I said flatly.

That stopped him.

"I found Eleanor's safety deposit box. I have a signed confession from James. He admitted Lila was pregnant. He admitted you helped him make her disappear."

Graham's jaw tightened. He moved to the window, one hand gripping the curtain.

"Eleanor's death wasn't natural, was it?" I asked quietly. "You silenced her before she could bring it public."

He turned. "You have no idea the damage she could have done."

"Damage?" Sam barked. "You call exposing a murder 'damage'?"

"She would've burned this town to the ground out of spite."

"No," I said. "She was trying to save it."

Graham's eyes met mine, tired and hollow. "You think anyone will believe you? That the town will turn on me? You don't understand how things work here."

"Maybe not," I said. "But the press does. And they'll print every word."

He smiled again, but it didn't reach his eyes. "Then you've already signed your own obituary."

Sam moved to my side. "We're not scared of you."

"You should be," Graham whispered.

I turned and walked out.

Sam followed close behind, but I knew the weight of those words would linger long after we left.

Back at Eleanor's, we found the back door ajar.

My pulse spiked. Sam pulled me behind him and stepped inside cautiously.

The living room was a mess. Couch overturned. Books scattered. The diary missing from the table.

"They were here," I breathed. "They took it."

Sam cursed under his breath. "They're trying to erase her again. And now us."

I sat heavily on the stairwell, trembling.

"But they don't know we sent everything to Jenna," I said. "They think the diary was the only thing."

Sam nodded. "They think they won. Let them."

I looked around the room—the remnants of Eleanor's life torn apart. But something deeper stirred in my chest now.

Not just grief. Or fear.

Resolve.

They carried the Hawthorne name like armor, but they'd forgotten one thing.

I carried Eleanor's legacy.

And I wasn't done yet.

Chapter 11 Missing Pages

The morning after the break-in, I found myself staring at the empty spot on the side table where Eleanor's diary used to sit. It felt like a physical absence, like a tooth pulled too soon—raw, tender, wrong.

"They didn't take anything else," Sam said, pacing near the kitchen window. "Not your laptop. Not the confession. Not even the envelope of photos."

"Just the diary," I murmured. "They knew exactly what to look for."

We'd stayed up most of the night reinforcing doors and windows. I barely slept. Every creak made me jolt. Every gust of wind sounded like footsteps.

"They must have been watching us closely," Sam said. "Maybe even inside the house. Before last night."

A sick feeling formed in my gut. "We have to assume everything in that diary is compromised."

"Not necessarily," Sam said. "You still have the copies of the key entries you scanned, right?"

"Yes, but not all of them," I said. "There were pages I flagged to read later. Things Eleanor wrote in code. She used a kind of shorthand only she and I understood—old family references, inside jokes."

Sam frowned. "And now they're gone."

I turned to the bookshelf beside the fireplace, eyes scanning titles. I pulled down *Wuthering Heights*, *The Bell Jar*, then paused on a thick, worn Bible. Inside, taped to the back cover, was a folded list—Eleanor's "index" to her coded entries. It was incomplete, handwritten in pencil, but it pointed to something I hadn't noticed before.

"Look at this," I said, spreading the list across the table. "She labeled the entries with numbers and single words. Like a code. '18: Hollow.' '26: Graham.' '31: Child.'"

Sam leaned in. "Entry 31 is gone, isn't it?"

I flipped through the scanned pages on my laptop. Entry 31 was missing—right between her last notes on Lila and the mention of the safety deposit box.

"Someone removed it before the break-in," I said slowly. "That page wasn't taken with the diary—it was already missing."

Sam looked at me. "Someone you trusted?"

I swallowed. "Maybe someone who knew exactly what Eleanor was onto. Someone who had access to the house."

The implications settled heavily between us.

Mrs. Graham. Detective Reynolds. Even Virginia.

"I need to go back to the church," I said. "There's a wall in the chapel covered in markings—symbols. One of them matched the carving at the tree."

"You think Eleanor left something there?"

"I think she revisited it a lot for a reason."

Sam stood, grabbing his coat. "Then I'm coming with you."

—

The chapel was empty when we arrived. The air was cool and heavy with the scent of candle wax and old wood. Sunlight filtered through the stained glass, casting muted reds and blues across the pews.

I walked to the back wall, near where I'd spoken with the elderly woman days ago. There, beneath a dusty hymn board, was the symbol: crescent and cross.

Sam joined me, and together we examined the area around it. I pressed against the panel, and with a soft creak, a section of the wooden wall loosened, revealing a hidden alcove no bigger than a shoebox.

Inside was a sealed envelope marked *For M.C.* in Eleanor's unmistakable script.

My heart skipped. "She left me a backup."

I opened it with trembling fingers. Inside was a photocopy of the missing diary entry.

Entry 31.
"Child."
Dated just a week before Eleanor's death.

"He told her she was carrying the future of the family—his words. That it wasn't a mistake, it was destiny. She cried when she said it, but I could see it: she loved that baby already. Said she wanted to keep it, no matter what. I promised to protect her. But she vanished the next day. If the child lived, it would be nearly 33 by now. But no records. No trace. Only a whisper. If the baby survived, someone hid them. And someone made damn sure the trail ended with me."

I sat back on my heels, stunned.

"She was pregnant," Sam said, voice hoarse. "And someone didn't just silence her. They erased her bloodline."

"Unless the child's still out there," I said.

A thought struck me like lightning.

"What if that's what Eleanor was really protecting? Not just Lila's story—but her child?"

Sam's expression darkened. "That's why the diary had to disappear. That entry links the Hawthornes not just to a disappearance—but to a living heir."

I stared down at the page. "That changes everything."

—

We drove back to Eleanor's house in silence, both of us replaying the implications.

In the foyer, we found the mail waiting on the table. A small envelope with no return address sat on top.

Inside was a single photo.

Lila.

Older.

She was standing in front of a bookstore, arm around a toddler. She looked healthy. Alive.

"Is this real?" Sam asked.

I turned the photo over. A scrawled note read:

You're getting close. Stop before someone else disappears.

My breath caught. "She survived."

"But someone doesn't want her found," Sam said.

I looked at the toddler again, at the shape of the child's eyes— striking, familiar.

My hands trembled. "That's the child."

Sam took the photo, examining the street signs in the background. "That's not Rosehill. That's... Pittsburgh. I recognize the storefront."

"We need to go," I said. "Now."

—

As we packed our bags, I checked the back door again—this time locking it twice. I couldn't shake the feeling that the walls were listening. That somewhere nearby, someone was watching, waiting.

We were close to the truth. Closer than Eleanor had ever been.

But the closer we got, the more dangerous everything became.

I clutched the photo to my chest and whispered under my breath.

"For you, Eleanor. For Lila. For the child they tried to erase."

And then we left the house behind us.

Headed toward answers.

And almost certainly, toward danger.

Chapter 12 Whispers of Witnesses

The road to Pittsburgh stretched out like a long breath held too tightly. The landscape blurred past the windows—rolling hills, skeletal trees, gray skies. I watched the world speed by in silence, the photo of Lila and the child resting in my lap like a sacred artifact.

"She lived," I whispered for the hundredth time. "She really lived."

Sam glanced at me, his hands steady on the steering wheel. "And the kid… if that's hers…"

"Then someone's spent decades hiding them," I said. "Either to protect them—or to control them."

It wasn't until we were halfway there that I realized I hadn't checked in with anyone since the break-in. No calls to Margot. No texts to anyone. If anything happened to us now, it might be days before anyone even noticed we were missing.

A thought that no longer felt like paranoia—but simple risk management.

We arrived just after noon.

The bookstore in the photo was tucked between a used clothing shop and a tattoo parlor in a quiet, artsy neighborhood. It looked exactly the same—green-painted bricks, a small sandwich board out front advertising author readings and herbal teas.

"I'll go in," I said. "You watch from across the street. If something feels off—leave. No questions."

Sam frowned. "You're not going in alone—"

"I am. This isn't Rosehill. If someone's watching us, they'll expect backup. Just… let me try this my way."

I crossed the street and entered the shop, the old brass bell above the door chiming softly.

Inside smelled like worn leather and lavender. The walls were lined with books on philosophy, herbalism, local poetry. A young woman with copper dreadlocks and cat-eye glasses sat at the register, typing on a laptop.

"Hi there," she said cheerily. "Looking for anything in particular?"

I hesitated. "I'm… actually looking for someone. She might've worked here, or been photographed here. This was taken about five or six years ago."

I slid the photo across the counter.

The woman frowned slightly, leaning in.

"Oh," she said. "Yeah. That's Sarah. She used to volunteer here. Ran our kids' reading hour for a while."

My heart jolted. "Do you know where she is now?"

She looked hesitant. "She moved. Left kind of suddenly. Around the time her kid started school."

"Do you remember where she went?"

The woman shook her head. "She didn't say. Just left a note thanking us for everything. Left behind a few boxes of books, actually. They're in the back if you want to look."

"Please."

She led me to a small storage room. Stacks of cardboard boxes were pushed into the corner. She pointed to two labeled *Sarah C.*

"I haven't gone through them," she said. "Figured she'd come back."

I opened the first box.

Journals. Notebooks. Kids' drawings. A few photos, mostly of nature, city walks, and the boy—older now, maybe five or six. He had Lila's eyes.

Then I found a library card tucked into a poetry book. The name read: **Sarah Carver.**

I looked up at the shopkeeper. "Can I borrow this box?"

She nodded, eyes wide now with curiosity. "Sure. You okay?"

"I don't know," I said honestly.

—

Back at the car, Sam scanned through the journals while I read Lila's handwriting—softer now, more fluid, but undeniably hers.

"She changed her name," he murmured. "Sarah Carver. Not exactly hiding hard."

"She wanted to be found—by the right people," I said. "Not the ones who hurt her."

One entry stood out.

October 3rd — He came into the store. I saw him. Older now. But it was him. I took the long way home and packed a bag. I've kept the boy safe for six years. I'll keep running if I have to. But I think they're closer than I thought.

My blood turned to ice.

"They found her again," I said. "And she ran. Again."

"But where?" Sam asked. "There's nothing else."

"Then we find someone who might've seen her."

—

We drove to the address listed on the library card—an apartment complex on the outskirts of the city. It was old, quiet, with cracked pavement and vines creeping up the balconies.

A woman in her sixties opened the door to the manager's office, eyeing us suspiciously.

"Can I help you?"

I showed her the library card and photo. "We're trying to find Sarah Carver. She used to live here."

She took the photo, her eyes softening with recognition.

"Sweet girl. And the boy—always polite. They left in a hurry. Must've been… maybe a year ago."

"Did she say where she was going?"

"No. But she left me this."

The woman reached behind the desk and handed me a sealed envelope. "Said if anyone ever came asking—someone who looked like they cared—I should give them this."

My hands trembled as I opened it.

Inside was a short note:

Maya, if it's you—thank you for finding me. I'm sorry I couldn't stay. I'm trying to protect him. Like Eleanor protected me. Please don't stop. But please don't follow, either. I need you alive to tell the story. It's the only way it ends.
– L

Below it was a single clue:
"Ask the bartender. He saw everything."

—

Sam and I stared at the note.

"The bartender?" he asked.

"The Maplewood Inn," I said. "Eleanor mentioned him in the diary. Said he hinted that he saw something the night Lila disappeared."

"Then that's where we go next."

I folded the letter carefully and tucked it away.

Lila had vanished again. But she had left behind a thread—a whisper, a witness.

We would follow it.

Even if it led straight into the lion's mouth.

Chapter 13 A Warning

The Maplewood Inn had always been the town's one dimly lit secret—the place where people went to be unseen. It didn't look like much from the outside: a squat building with a battered sign, flickering neon beer ads in the windows, and a parking lot filled with dusty pickup trucks and rusted sedans.

Sam and I walked in just before dusk. The air inside was heavy with cigarette smoke, the scent of stale beer and old wood thick in the walls. A low hum of conversation buzzed from the back, but most heads turned when we entered. Outsiders were easy to spot in Rosehill—even ones who used to belong.

The bartender was a broad-shouldered man in his sixties with salt-and-pepper stubble and a deep crease between his brows. He looked up from wiping down a glass and met my eyes.

"You're Eleanor Carter's girl," he said—not a question, a statement.

"Yes," I replied. "I'm looking for answers."

He nodded once and pointed toward the far end of the bar, where the shadows pooled thickest.

"Sit."

We did.

He poured two glasses of water without asking, then leaned forward, arms crossed on the counter. "You came here 'cause of Lila."

"Yes," I said. "You knew her."

"I did." He sighed. "Whole damn town did."

"You saw her the night she disappeared."

His jaw worked for a moment. "I did."

Sam leaned in. "You told Eleanor. She wrote it in her diary."

He nodded. "Didn't think anyone else would ever come asking."

"I'm not here to stir up gossip," I said. "I'm here to tell the truth. I have her letter. I know about James. I know about the pregnancy. And I know Eleanor died trying to protect that story."

He gave a low whistle. "So you do know."

"Tell me what you saw," I said.

He wiped his hands on a bar towel, his eyes growing distant.

"Summer of '87. Lila came in crying. Not drunk, not high—just scared. She sat right where you're sitting now. Said she couldn't go home. Said she had to leave town. Asked if I knew anyone who could drive her as far as Pittsburgh. I offered to call someone I trusted."

"Who?" I asked.

"Truck driver named Carl. Quiet guy, no connections to Rosehill. Did favors sometimes for kids trying to get out. I went to the back to use the payphone, and when I came back—she was gone."

My stomach sank. "Gone?"

"Gone. Just like that. No goodbye. No thank you. Like someone pulled her out of the bar."

"Did you see anyone?"

He hesitated. "Not at first. But I asked around. A waitress said she saw a black Lincoln parked outside—engine running. One of those older models, the kind the councilmen used to drive."

"James Hawthorne?" I asked.

"Or Graham. Or both."

My hands clenched. "And you didn't tell the police?"

"I did. You think they listened?" He leaned closer. "I tried. I tried again when Eleanor came asking, years later. They told me to drop it. Even threatened to pull my liquor license."

I swallowed hard. "So you stayed silent."

"I thought I was keeping people safe," he said. "Turns out I was just keeping them scared."

Sam spoke up. "It's not too late. You can still tell your story."

He shook his head. "You don't get it, do you? You're poking a bear that never learned to sleep. These people—what they did—it wasn't just about Lila. It was about protecting their name. Their legacy."

"We know that," I said. "But the truth—her truth—deserves air."

He looked at me for a long moment. "Eleanor used to say that too."

"She was right."

He reached under the bar and pulled out a worn envelope. "I never had the nerve to give this to her. I wrote everything down after that night. Who I saw. What I heard. Names. Timelines. I was waiting for someone brave enough to take it."

He slid it to me.

"This is the last I'll say. And when you leave here—you didn't see me."

I nodded. "Thank you."

He gave me a sad smile. "Just be careful. Last time someone tried to tell this story, she ended up buried under a clean coroner's report."

—

Outside, the air was cold. Sharp. The sky had turned the color of ash.

We didn't speak until we were back at the car. I tore open the envelope and scanned the contents.

It was a statement—handwritten and detailed.

Lila. Her arrival. Her fear. The black car. The names James and Graham. Even a timestamp. And at the bottom, his signature.

Sam exhaled. "This is it. This could crack everything wide open."

"Or get us killed," I said.

We drove back to Eleanor's house in silence.

But as we pulled into the driveway, we saw something that made my heart stop.

The front door was wide open.

Sam slammed the car into park.

We rushed inside—calling out, checking every room.

Nothing was missing.

Except one thing.

The scanned copy of the confession—gone from my laptop. Deleted. Wiped.

They had been inside again.

Sam checked the logs. "They accessed the files through the Wi-Fi. Remote access. Someone's been watching your system."

I sat on the floor, stunned. "They're one step ahead."

"No," he said. "We still have the bartender's statement. We still have the letter from Lila. We still have the truth."

"But they're coming faster now," I said. "They're getting desperate."

Sam looked me dead in the eyes. "Good. That means they're scared."

I nodded.

But deep down, I was starting to wonder:

How many warnings could we ignore before one of them finally came true?

Chapter 14 The Tree Symbol

It was Sam who suggested we go back to the woods.

"This isn't just about evidence anymore," he said, pulling on his coat. "Eleanor marked the tree for a reason. Maybe what she couldn't write down, she left behind."

The words had lingered with me all night. I barely slept, replaying the timeline of Lila's disappearance in my mind. Over and over, it led back to the same place—Greenhill Campground. The bent tree. The crescent and cross. The carving that had marked the place where Lila was last seen.

But what if that symbol meant more than we thought?

What if it wasn't just a mark?

What if it was a map?

—

We hiked out early the next morning, the air sharp with autumn and the sky overcast. The woods had a hush to them—a stillness that seemed too deliberate.

We reached the tree an hour later.

It looked exactly the same: bent trunk, ancient roots gripping the earth, the crescent-and-cross carving weathered but visible.

I circled the base, hand trailing across the bark. "Eleanor wrote about this tree in at least three entries. Said it was the last place Lila was seen. But also something else…"

I pulled out my notebook and flipped to the relevant excerpt.

"The roots remember what the branches forget. Dig at the second curve. Beneath stone and shadow, the truth sleeps."

Sam crouched next to me. "Second curve. That must mean the second bend in the roots."

We began clearing away fallen leaves, using small hand shovels from his backpack. The soil was damp and dense. Minutes passed. Then—

"Here," Sam said. He tapped something hard.

I reached down and brushed away more earth.

It was a wooden box.

Old. Warped by moisture, but intact.

Together, we pried it open.

Inside was a smaller, sealed container—watertight plastic. And inside that, wrapped in wax paper and velvet, were three items: a small notebook, a flash drive, and a photograph.

The photo was of Eleanor and Lila, standing beside the tree, smiling. Lila's hand rested gently on her abdomen.

"She was already pregnant," I whispered.

Sam picked up the flash drive. "We'll need to check this somewhere secure."

But the notebook—the notebook stopped everything.

It was Eleanor's.

Written in tiny, deliberate handwriting was what appeared to be her final record. Her last attempt to preserve the truth.

We sat against the roots and began to read aloud, alternating entries.

"They threatened me directly today. Said I needed to stop 'digging up old graves.' Said if I didn't, people might start thinking I was unstable. That I'd be 'better off resting.'"

I pressed the notebook to my chest, overwhelmed.

"She knew," I said. "She knew they'd come for her."

Sam looked toward the horizon, where the trees gave way to the edge of Rosehill. "And she still chose to keep going."

We buried the box again, sealing it tight before covering it with leaves and stone. A hidden record, should anything happen to us.

As we hiked back toward the car, the wind picked up, shaking the branches overhead.

But it didn't feel ominous.

It felt like a voice.

A whisper.

Like Eleanor, still watching.

Still guiding.

Back at the house, we plugged the flash drive into Sam's encrypted laptop.

Inside were two folders.

One was labeled **"SCANS – CONFIDENTIAL"**. The other: **"ROSEHILL RECORDINGS."**

We opened the first.

Hundreds of scanned documents appeared on the screen—copies of pages from Eleanor's diary, Lila's school records, a birth certificate dated 1988 with the child's name blacked out.

And then—an arrest report.

But not for Lila.

For James Hawthorne.

1987.   Two weeks before Lila disappeared.

Assault of a minor. Dismissed by town council.

Sam read it twice. "This was buried. Completely. No public record. It's a miracle Eleanor found this."

"She didn't just find it," I said. "She risked everything to preserve it."

The second folder contained audio.

Recordings Eleanor had taken—of her own conversations.

The first file clicked on.

ELEANOR (tired, calm): "You're threatening me."

MALE VOICE (calm, calculated): "I'm warning you. Walk away from this, and you'll live long enough to regret it."

ELEANOR: "No. I'll die knowing I was right."

Sam looked at me, stunned. "That's Graham Hawthorne."

I nodded. "And now we have his voice saying exactly what he denied for decades."

We copied the files onto three flash drives, then encrypted and uploaded everything to secure cloud storage.

"It's time to send this to Jenna," I said.

Sam nodded. "And then what?"

"Then we publish it ourselves. If anything happens to us, the world still finds out."

He looked at me with something like admiration—and maybe fear. "You're ready for war."

I stared out the window, toward the woods we'd just returned from.

"No," I said quietly. "I'm finishing one."

—

That night, I lit a candle for Eleanor and placed it on the kitchen windowsill.

Outside, the wind howled through the trees.

But I wasn't afraid anymore.

Not of shadows. Not of legacies.

Not even of the Hawthornes.

The tree had given us its truth.

And I was going to make damn sure the world heard it.

Chapter 15 Sam Disappears

The sun rose gray and heavy the next morning, its light thin and watery as it bled through the curtains. It should have been a moment of triumph. We had the files, the photos, the voices of the dead and damned alike. Proof of everything Eleanor died trying to expose.

But when I came downstairs, the couch was empty.

No rumpled blankets. No coffee mug. No laptop. Just an echoing absence.

"Sam?" I called out, my voice louder than I expected.

Silence.

I checked the kitchen. The door was locked from the inside. No signs of a break-in. No message. His shoes were still by the mat. His bag was still leaning against the coat rack.

But he was gone.

Panic surged in my chest, clawing its way up my throat.

I tried calling his phone. It rang twice. Then went straight to voicemail.

I tried again. Same thing.

Something was wrong. Deeply wrong.

I raced to the desk and opened our shared file folders—everything we'd collected, copied, documented. The digital backups were still there. Password protected. Nothing had been tampered with.

But there was no trace of Sam.

Just the lingering scent of his cologne in the air. And a single piece of paper left neatly on the coffee table.

One word written in block letters:

"STOP."

—

I drove to the library first.

The doors were locked. Sam's car wasn't in the lot.

I banged on the back entrance anyway, shouting his name.

Nothing.

The archivist, a nervous young man named Peter, eventually opened the door, clearly startled. "Maya? What's going on?"

"Sam," I said breathlessly. "Have you seen him today?"

"No," he said. "He called in. Said he wasn't coming."

"When?"

Peter checked his phone. "Around six this morning."

That was hours ago.

"Did he say why?"

"He didn't sound like himself," Peter said. "Just said something about needing to take care of something. Then hung up."

I ran.

—

Next stop: the police station.

Reynolds wasn't at the front desk. The woman on duty gave me a wary look as I explained the situation.

"We can't file a missing person report until twenty-four hours have passed," she said flatly.

"He's not missing," I snapped. "He's taken. Or forced to run."

Her eyes narrowed. "You have proof of that?"

"I have a note," I said, thrusting it toward her. "Left at my house. In all caps. 'STOP.' That's not something Sam would write. Not like that."

She took it with disinterest. "We'll make a record. But it's probably nothing. You two have been stirring things up. Maybe he just needed space."

I leaned across the desk. "If anything happens to him—and I mean anything—I'll hold this whole town responsible. And this time, there will be consequences."

She didn't reply.

I turned and left before I said something worse.

—

Back at the house, the silence was unbearable.

Every creak made my skin crawl.

I checked the flash drives again. Still there. Still intact.

But that wasn't what mattered anymore.

What mattered was that Sam was gone. And I had no idea who had him—or what they planned to do with him.

I sat on the floor beside Eleanor's fireplace, heart pounding.

Was this what she felt in her final days? That slow unraveling of safety? That awareness that the net was tightening?

I checked the hidden archive Eleanor had kept beneath the loose floorboard in her study. Still there. But even its presence felt like ashes in my hands.

Without Sam, it meant nothing.

Without Sam, I was alone.

And that terrified me more than the Hawthornes ever could.

—

That night, I drove aimlessly for hours.

I circled the old church, the cemetery, the diner. Even Greenhill Campground. I checked every familiar place, every backroad we'd taken together, every place Eleanor had ever mentioned.

I whispered his name to the trees.

Nothing answered.

At midnight, I returned to the house and found a letter taped to the front door.

Typed.

"You were warned. This is not a story. It is a bloodline. Drop the files. Or the boy dies."

I crumpled it in my fist, fury boiling in my chest.

Not just fear. Fury.

They had taken Sam.

They had made this personal.

But what they didn't understand—what they would never understand—was that Eleanor raised me better than that. She didn't raise me to run.

She raised me to fight.

And now I would fight with everything I had.

—

I drove straight to Virginia's cottage.

It was nearly 1 a.m., but the lights were still on.

She answered the door before I could knock, as though she had been waiting for me.

"You know," I said.

She nodded. "They have him."

"Where?"

"I don't know," she said. "But I know how they work. The Hawthornes don't kill unless they have to. They threaten. Intimidate. Try to make you give up on your own."

"He's not giving up," I said. "And neither am I."

Virginia motioned me inside. Her living room smelled of mint tea and old wood. The same as the first night.

She sat heavily and pulled out a worn notebook. "Your aunt left me one last message. I never showed you before because… well, I didn't think you were ready. Now I'm not sure anyone is."

She handed me a page torn from the back.

"If they take someone, follow the paper. The paper always leaves a trail. Ownership. Trusts. Secret ledgers. Everything is hidden in names—but names are paper, and paper burns. But not before it leaves smoke."

"Smoke," I whispered. "Financial records."

Virginia nodded. "There's a Hawthorne shell company listed on the deed to an old boarding house. It's been closed for years. Out past the old mill road. They used it back in the day to 'reform' troubled teens."

"Do you think he's there?"

"I think it's the kind of place no one would hear him scream."

I stood. "Then that's where I go."

Virginia grabbed my wrist. "You can't go alone."

"I already am."

Her grip tightened. "Then take this."

She handed me a small silver revolver wrapped in a handkerchief.

I stared at it, heart pounding.

"I pray you won't need it," she said. "But if you do, don't hesitate."

—

An hour later, I stood outside the abandoned boarding house.

Its windows were boarded, the roof sagging, the porch swallowed by weeds.

But a single light glowed from an upstairs window.

I gripped the revolver tighter.

"Hold on, Sam," I whispered.

And I stepped into the darkness.

Chapter 16 Accusation

I didn't think it could get worse after Sam vanished.

I was wrong.

The morning after his disappearance, I returned to the library hoping for answers—but instead found whispers, stares, and a single officer waiting outside the doors with his hand on his hip and a grim expression on his face.

"Maya Carter?" he asked.

"Yes."

"You'll need to come with me."

"For what?"

"Questions regarding Sam Wilcox."

I blinked. "He's missing."

"Yes," he said slowly. "And some people seem to think you had something to do with that."

The world tilted slightly.

"You think I—? No. No, I'm the one who's been looking for him. He was staying with me."

"We're aware. Come on. Let's not make a scene."

The interrogation room at the Rosehill police station was colder than it had any right to be. Fluorescent lights buzzed overhead like insects trapped behind glass. I sat on one side of a metal table, a paper cup of water untouched before me. Detective Reynolds finally entered, closing the door with a soft click.

He didn't sit.

Instead, he dropped a folder onto the table and stared down at me like I was a puzzle he wasn't sure how to solve.

"You said you were with Sam the night he disappeared," he began.

"I was," I said, voice steady. "We were working on the Hawthorne case."

"You say that like it's still open."

"It should be."

He opened the folder and pulled out a photograph.

It was of me—standing in front of Eleanor's house the night before Sam went missing, flashlight in one hand, the revolver Virginia gave me tucked visibly into my coat.

"Why are you carrying a weapon?" he asked.

"For protection. After the files were leaked. After the tire-slashing. After the break-in. Do I need to keep going?"

He didn't flinch.

"Neighbors say they heard shouting. That you and Sam were arguing. That you were angry."

My mouth went dry. "That's not what happened."

"Then tell me what did."

I hesitated. Not because I didn't know. But because suddenly, for the first time, I wasn't sure Reynolds believed me.

"We had a lead," I said. "We were going to follow it. When I woke up the next morning, he was gone. Just gone. No note, no text. Just… nothing."

Reynolds narrowed his eyes. "And you didn't come to the police?"

"I did. Your desk sergeant told me to wait twenty-four hours."

He closed the folder.

"Here's the thing, Maya," he said. "You and Sam have been digging into old ghosts. You've pissed off powerful people. I don't know if what you're doing is brave or reckless. But I do know this—people who cross lines tend to get blamed when things go wrong."

"So you're blaming me?" I asked quietly.

"I'm saying that right now, the town is whispering. And when Rosehill whispers long enough, it turns into something worse."

He slid a release form across the table.

"We're holding you overnight while we investigate. For your safety and others'. But if anything happens to Sam—if we find any evidence connecting you—you're going to need a lawyer."

He left without another word.

I stared at the door long after it clicked shut.

They were turning this on me. All of it. Erasing the truth by flipping the narrative.

And if I didn't find Sam soon, they'd bury me with the rest of it.

The cell was small. Cinderblock walls. Metal cot. A single toilet in the corner.

They didn't charge me.

They didn't need to.

The accusation was enough.

I lay awake, staring at the ceiling, retracing every step of the past few days. Somewhere in the shadows of Rosehill, Sam was hurt. Or hiding. Or worse. And now I was locked away, silenced the way Eleanor had been—through doubt.

But I wouldn't break.

Not here.

Not now.

The next morning, the officer returned. "You're being released."

I stood slowly. "What changed?"

He hesitated, then handed me a phone.

There was a message from Jenna.

Check your inbox. Sam's alive.
But you need to move. Fast.

Chapter 17 Eleanor's Past

The rain had returned.

It tapped steadily against the windows of Eleanor's study, soft but relentless. Outside, the branches swayed like they remembered something. The house groaned with the weight of history, and I knew that whatever came next—I needed to understand where it all began.

Sam was safe now, recovering at Jenna's apartment out of town. The trial loomed, but we'd bought time. Time to breathe. Time to think.

Time to finish what Eleanor started.

I sat alone at Eleanor's desk that afternoon, the storm outside a mirror to the one still cracking inside me. The diary was gone, the first copy burned in the fire of secrecy. But the copies, the backups, the boxes in the attic—I still had those.

And something inside me whispered that I had missed something important.

Something deeply personal.

I climbed to the attic and pulled down the faded green trunk that had sat untouched in the corner since Eleanor's passing. Dust coated the surface, and its brass latches clicked like old bones as I opened them.

Inside were stacks of photographs bundled with twine, postcards, old appointment books, and a few vinyl records with handwritten labels: *Autumn Mix, Storm Songs, For Lila.*

That was the first time I cried.

Not out of grief. But recognition.

She hadn't just mourned Lila.

She had loved her.

Truly. Deeply.

There, in the bottom of the trunk, were dozens of photos—many I had never seen before. Not the kind you frame, but the kind you tuck away because they're too precious to risk fading.

Eleanor and Lila—arms slung around each other, laughing over ice cream cones. Standing in front of the tree. Sitting cross-legged on the floor of Eleanor's old dorm, surrounded by records and teacups.

In one, Lila had her hand on Eleanor's cheek, as if caught in mid-laugh. In another, they were sitting in the back of a pickup truck under a blanket, watching fireworks.

The dates on the back ranged from 1985 to early 1987.

Before it all fell apart.

Before Lila vanished.

I sat on the floor, spreading them out around me like pieces of a puzzle, a life remembered in fragments.

And I began to see the truth.

Not just about what happened.

But about who Eleanor really was.

—

She hadn't just tried to protect Lila because she was kind. Or stubborn. Or curious.

She had done it because she loved her.

Because maybe, in another version of the world, they had a future together—one not defined by fear and power and legacy.

I found a letter, tucked between the folds of a photo album.

It was never sent.

Lila,
I don't know if you're alive. I don't know if you ever read this. But I need you to know—I tried. I tried so hard. They told me I was crazy. That you ran. That you never loved me. But I remember the way you looked at me under that damn tree. I remember the way you held my hand after the council meeting. And I remember you whispering that the baby wasn't a curse—it was yours. Yours to keep. Yours to love. And I believed you.
If you're alive—don't forgive me. Just know that I never stopped looking. Not for a moment.
—Eleanor

I pressed the letter to my chest and closed my eyes.

So much had been taken from them. From Eleanor. From Lila. From the child they never got to raise together. But this letter—these photos—they were proof that even in the darkest corners of this town, love had bloomed. Quietly. Fiercely.

And maybe that's what scared the Hawthornes most of all.

Not the truth.

But the love beneath it.

The kind they could never control.

—

I placed the photographs carefully into a new binder and labeled it simply:
Eleanor + Lila

It wasn't evidence.

It was remembrance.

It was the heart of the storm.

The thing worth fighting for.

—

Downstairs, I called Elise.

"I found them," I said.

"Found who?" she asked, gently.

"Our mothers."

She didn't speak for a long time. Then, "I'd like to see."

"You will," I said. "I'll show you everything."

—

As the rain faded and the dusk settled, I placed the binder on Eleanor's writing table.

Not hidden.

Not buried.

But displayed, waiting for the world to see.

Because some truths didn't belong in police files or trial exhibits.

They belonged in plain sight.

Chapter 18 Safety Deposit Key

It began with a book.

Or, more precisely, it began with a book falling from a shelf.

I was in Eleanor's study late one night, reorganizing. Not because it needed organizing, but because I needed the noise, the motion—

anything to quiet the low thrum of adrenaline that had refused to fade since the trial began.

It was a leather-bound copy of *Middlemarch,* heavy with time and swollen from damp. I had pulled a handful of volumes from the shelf and was stacking them in neat piles when the book slipped, struck the floor, and cracked open with a sound too sharp for paper alone.

A small thud echoed inside the cover.

I froze.

My first thought was absurd: a mouse? A dried flower? But when I picked the book up, I realized the spine felt… uneven. Lumpy.

I pried it further apart.

And that's when I saw it.

A slit, delicately made, in the thick cardboard beneath the spine's leather covering. And wedged inside—so tightly that I had to wiggle it free with a letter opener—was a tiny, tarnished brass key.

My heart began to race.

Attached to it with brittle twine was a tag. I unfolded it slowly.

In Eleanor's unmistakable hand:

Safety Deposit Box — 217, Rosehill Bank
"In case they take everything else."

I stared at it, stunned.

All this time—after flash drives, tree roots, recordings, court evidence—there had still been one more card left in Eleanor's hand.

And she had hidden it in the one place no one would look: inside a book she read every winter, a story of complexity and truth, of women who knew too much and were punished for it.

It was so perfectly her that I smiled through my shock.

The safety deposit box must have been something separate from the earlier one I'd accessed. Something even more private. Something Eleanor had only intended to be found if everything else was gone.

And now, it was mine.

—

The next morning, I was the first person through the doors of Rosehill Bank.

The teller recognized me immediately, her smile flickering like a broken neon sign. She must have seen the headlines. Everyone had. But she said nothing, just nodded when I showed the key.

"I'll need to see some identification," she said quietly.

I handed over my license and the key together. She examined both, then motioned to a security guard, who led me through a heavy door and down a narrow hall.

We stopped in front of a vault lined with small silver boxes.

"Box 217," the guard said, gesturing.

The key slid into the lock with a satisfying click.

Inside was a small, velvet-lined container. On top sat a sealed envelope and beneath it—what looked like an old cassette tape and a flash drive. I carried the whole box to a private viewing room and locked the door behind me.

I opened the envelope first.

The letter inside was long. Eleanor's handwriting, even at the end, remained steady, if smaller than I remembered.

Maya,
If you've found this, then they took everything else. Which means

you're still fighting. Which means I was right about you.
There were things I couldn't put in the diary. Couldn't say out loud.
Not because I didn't want to—but because I needed to protect
people. Not just Lila. But others.
The flash drive contains records from the Hawthorne Trust. Off-
the-books payments. Real estate deeds. Names. Donations. Some of
it goes beyond Rosehill. The roots stretch into Harrisburg. Even
DC. It's not just about Lila anymore. It never was.
The tape is different. That's for you. I recorded it the night I made
peace with the fact that I might not survive this.
Listen to it when you're ready. Not before.
And the final document—beneath the lining—isn't for the court. It's
not for reporters. It's for Elise.
It proves everything she ever wondered about her mother. And it's
written in Lila's own hand.
Guard it with your life.
Always,
Eleanor

My hands shook.

I took a slow breath, then lifted the lining of the box.

Taped beneath it was a folded sheet of thick paper. Faded. The edges fraying.

I opened it carefully.

It was a letter.

To my daughter,
If someone is reading this, it means I couldn't stay. I wanted to.
More than anything. But they were watching. Always watching.
And I had to keep you safe.
You were not a mistake. You were my miracle.
I loved your father once. But he changed. Power changed him. And
when he said you would ruin everything, I knew I had to run.
But I want you to know something that matters more than any

I sat there for a long time, silent.

The hum of the vault echoed faintly outside the door.

The sun filtered in through a thin slit of glass.

And for the first time since Eleanor's death, I felt like I could
finally breathe.

—

That evening, I drove to Elise's house.

She opened the door before I could knock.

"I have something," I said.

She didn't ask what. Just stepped aside and let me in.

We sat in her kitchen, the light low, her son asleep upstairs.

I handed her the letter.

Her hands trembled as she unfolded it. As her eyes scanned the
words, her breath caught. Once. Twice.

Then she pressed it to her chest and closed her eyes.

"She chose me," she whispered.

"She did," I said. "Every time."

Elise didn't cry. She just nodded, over and over, like someone
receiving a truth they had waited their entire life to believe.

After a while, she looked up.

"Thank you," she said.

"You don't have to thank me."

"Yes, I do," she said. "You could have stopped. You didn't. You made sure this didn't disappear like they wanted."

She reached across the table and took my hand.

"I think she would've loved you," she added.

"Eleanor?" I asked.

"No," Elise said. "My mother."

—

I didn't listen to the tape for another two days.

When I finally did, I waited until it was raining again. The kind of rain that turned windows into watercolor paintings. I lit a candle, poured tea, and slid the cassette into the old player I found in Eleanor's attic.

The tape clicked. Then hissed.

And then her voice.

Soft. Tired. But sure.

"If you're listening, then I'm gone. And that's alright. I made peace with that a long time ago. But you should know the full story."

She spoke of Lila first.

Of their early friendship. Their slow-burning affection. The first time she realized she wanted to protect Lila not because she felt responsible, but because she was in love.

She spoke of the fear, the night Lila found out she was pregnant, the whisper that she was planning to run. She spoke of watching Lila slip through the cracks, unable to save her, and of how she had dedicated the rest of her life to making sure her story didn't die with her.

"I knew they'd call me paranoid. They always do, when women don't shut up. But I never cared what they thought. I cared what she would've thought. What you would think, someday."

Her voice caught once. Then steadied.

"So if you're listening, Maya, it means I did the right thing. I picked the right person. Not because you're perfect. But because you finish things. Even when they're impossible. Even when they hurt."

There was a pause.

Then the tape ended.

I sat in silence for a long time.

Not because I didn't know what to feel.

But because I felt everything.

—

Later that night, I added the key and the letter to a small wooden box I kept in Eleanor's study—my study now. The fireplace flickered beside me. A journal lay open on the desk, a fresh page ready to receive whatever came next.

I wrote three words.

She chose truth.

And then beneath them:

So will I.

Chapter 19 The Final Entry

It took me three days to return to Eleanor's journal.

Not because I'd forgotten it. No—its presence on the corner of her old writing desk was impossible to ignore. The deep green leather cover had grown familiar to me, the pages so saturated with pain and courage that I could practically feel the pulse of her thoughts just beneath the spine.

I waited because I wasn't ready.

Because some truths, even when known, still need time to settle in the chest before they're spoken aloud.

But on the fourth morning—when the autumn wind rattled the windows and the air smelled faintly of pine and smoke—I returned to the study. To her desk. To the final page.

The last entry in Eleanor's handwriting had been written with precision. The ink steady, the words careful. She had known it might be her last.

And yet—beneath it, tucked neatly between the final page and the back cover, was another sheet of paper.

A single folded letter, hidden flat against the binding.

With trembling fingers, I unfolded it.

It wasn't dated. It wasn't titled.

But I knew what it was.

It was the confession.

If you're reading this, then they haven't silenced me the way they wanted to. Not entirely.

You've made it further than anyone else ever did. Even me. And I think that means you deserve the truth. The whole of it.

Her name was Lila Carver. She was 17 when I met her. Sharp. Kind. Closed off in the way that girls learn to be when the world teaches them early that beauty is dangerous.

She was brilliant. And she was so, so lonely.

They tried to make it a scandal. Later, after she disappeared. Said I'd "taken an interest." That I'd lost perspective. But the truth was simple, and too big for them to understand: I loved her.

We were together. Quietly. Fiercely. The way you are when you don't think you'll get a second chance.

Then she told me she was pregnant.

It was James Hawthorne. Of course it was. A moment of trust she had come to regret. A mistake. A crime, even. But Lila didn't speak in terms of victims and villains. She spoke in realities. She said she wanted the baby. Said she would raise it with or without his name attached.

That was when everything changed.

She came to me crying one night. Said James knew. That his uncle Graham had threatened her. That if she didn't leave town quietly, things would happen. To her. To me.

We made a plan to run. I bought two bus tickets to Pittsburgh. We packed bags.

The night before we were supposed to leave, she vanished.

The police said she ran. Everyone else said she snapped. That I snapped. That I'd imagined the whole thing.

But I knew. I knew something had happened. I could feel the absence like an amputation.

And so I started collecting everything I could find. Letters. Photos. Notes. Hearsay. Whispers.

The picture they painted was too consistent to be coincidence.

She didn't run.

She was erased.

Because the truth—her child—was a threat to the Hawthorne name.

And when people like that feel threatened, they don't argue.

They bury.

I sat back, the confession spread across my lap, my hands trembling.

This was no longer just about the facts. The investigation. The trial. The whispers in the corners of Rosehill. This was the soul of it. The raw, vulnerable truth Eleanor had never dared to say aloud.

She had loved Lila.

They had loved each other.

And that love had been buried under lies for thirty years.

I carefully refolded the page and placed it back where I had found it, smoothing the cover of the journal with reverent fingers.

Then I reached for my own pen.

Because the story wasn't done yet.

Entry 50
October 31st
Rosehill

This is the final entry.

Not because the story has ended, but because the silence has.

I found Eleanor's confession.

Not the kind that asks forgiveness. Not the kind a priest might record. But a declaration. Of love. Of purpose. Of defiance.

She and Lila were in love. That was the truth.

Not rumor. Not theory. Truth.

It was a love that bloomed in the shadow of a town built on control. And when that love threatened the Hawthornes' illusion of order, they struck.

They made Lila disappear.

They turned Eleanor into a madwoman.

And they thought that would be enough.

But it wasn't.

Because Eleanor kept writing.

Because I came back.

Because Sam believed.

Because Elise survived.

And because truth, even when hidden, leaves a trail.

The trial is over. Graham Hawthorne will spend the rest of his days behind bars. James disappeared decades ago, likely aided by the very same network that paid for silence at every level of this town. But his shame—his crime—is now known.

Lila's daughter—Elise—is living proof of what they tried to erase.

And now, Eleanor's name is not a warning, or a joke, or a slur whispered behind hands.

It's a banner.

A flame.

They called her the Widow.

Said she lived in that house too long. Said she walked too quietly. Said she kept her curtains drawn and wrote too many letters.

But I know better now.

Eleanor wasn't mourning a man.

She was mourning a world that had no space for her truth.

She didn't weep in corners or wear black.

She turned grief into pages.

And ink into armor.

I live in her house now.

I wake in the room where she once dreamed.

I cook in the kitchen where she once washed dishes with Lila by her side.

I sit at her desk and look out at the same twisted tree.

And sometimes, when the wind is just right, I swear I hear her voice.

Not in words.

But in knowing.

A quiet sense that I am not alone.

That I have joined the line of women who refused to vanish.

So here is my final entry.

Not because the pages have run out.

But because the torch has been passed.

To Elise.

To her son.

To anyone who finds this journal and understands that the past does not stay buried unless we let it.

Eleanor chose to stay and fight.

Lila chose to run and protect.

I chose to return and uncover.

We are not the same.

But we are all the same kind of woman.

The kind who keeps going.

The kind who leaves a record.

If you're reading this—whoever you are—remember that secrets are like seeds.

You can bury them.

But if the soil is rich enough, and someone is willing to water them with truth—

They will grow.

Even in darkness.

Especially in darkness.

This was Eleanor's journal.

Now, it is yours.

Use it well.

Chapter 20 Breaking In

There was something intimate about opening a box you weren't supposed to find.

It wasn't like discovering a diary or stumbling onto a hidden photograph. This wasn't an accidental secret. This was a deliberate one—a confession so carefully buried that only one key, one person, and one precise moment could unlock it.

That person was me.

And that moment had come.

Eleanor had written a cryptic phrase in one of her last letters: *"In case they take everything else, go to 1843."*

For weeks, I assumed it was metaphorical. A date. A verse. But tucked inside a book in her bedroom—*Wuthering Heights*, dog-eared and fraying—I found a business card with a code scrawled on the back.

Box 1843 – Rosehill First National Bank.
Access granted upon verification of Eleanor's estate.

I held the card like it might combust in my hand.

Sam stood behind me. "That's not the same deposit box you accessed last month?"

"No," I said. "That one was listed in the will. This one… wasn't."

He raised an eyebrow. "Then she didn't want the lawyers to find it."

"Exactly," I said, sliding the card into my pocket. "And now we're going to find out why."

The bank was quiet when we arrived.

It always was—a cold, polished place where everything seemed too white, too sterile. The kind of place where secrets pretended to wear suits and pay taxes.

The clerk looked up as I approached the counter. A young man, fresh-faced and nervous.

"I need access to a safety deposit box," I said, trying to keep my voice calm. "Box 1843. I have the key and the paperwork."

He blinked. "That's… a restricted box. I've never processed one that high before."

"It's under Eleanor Carter's estate. Here's the court order verifying I'm the executor."

He took the documents, mouth twitching slightly. "Give me a moment."

As he disappeared into the back, I turned to Sam.

"If this goes wrong—"

"It won't," he said, cutting me off. "But if it does, I've got a backup plan."

I smiled weakly. "Always the pragmatist."

"Always the one who wants you alive."

The clerk returned, hands slightly trembling.

"You're authorized. Please follow me."

—

The vault was deeper than I expected. The hallway was long, sterile, lined with identical boxes. Box 1843 was the only one with a black faceplate. The number etched in silver. Unassuming. Quiet.

Just like Eleanor.

The clerk unlocked the outer mechanism and stepped back.

"You may use the private viewing room," he said, avoiding eye contact.

Inside the room, the lights were warm. The walls were soundproofed. A surveillance camera blinked slowly in the corner.

I placed the box on the table and took a breath.

Then I opened it.

Inside was… not what I expected.

There was no envelope of cash. No thick folder of documents. No revolver or confession.

Instead, there were three items.

1. A slim leather-bound ledger.

2. A cassette tape in a plastic case labeled *"For Maya – Play Alone."*

3. A thick, sealed manila envelope marked: **"For Attorney General's Office – Only in Case of My Death."**

My stomach dropped.

I picked up the ledger first.

Inside, it was a ledger of names, dates, and transactions. Handwritten, precise, like everything Eleanor did. But the names weren't Rosehill's usual suspects.

These were state officials. Lobbyists. A judge. A U.S. Congressman.

Each entry was paired with a dollar amount, a note, and a symbol: H, G, or both.

Hawthorne.

Graham.

Sometimes both.

At the bottom of the final page, in Eleanor's handwriting:

"If the town won't believe in rot, show them the roots. This isn't just about Lila. It's about power. Power bought with blood."

I felt sick.

I had known the Hawthornes were corrupt. But this—this was national. Systemic. A tree whose limbs stretched far beyond Rosehill.

I handed the ledger to Sam.

His eyes widened. "This… this could take down more than a family."

"Which is why she kept it here," I said. "And why no one could find it unless they were willing to look deeper than the town's guilt."

I turned to the cassette tape.

Sam reached for it, but I stopped him.

"She said play it alone."

He hesitated, then nodded. "I'll wait outside."

—

I pressed PLAY.

Eleanor's voice filled the room.

Soft. Clear. Steady.

"If you're hearing this, then I'm gone. Not missing. Not mad. Gone. And if I'm gone, it means I finally pushed too far."

"You've likely seen the ledger. The names. The money. I've spent thirty years collecting it. Hiding it. Praying I'd never have to use it."

"But Maya, if this tape is in your hands, then it's time."

There was a pause. A breath.

"They didn't just kill Lila. They built careers off her silence. Used the money meant to keep her hidden to fund campaigns, buy judges, protect predators. What happened in Rosehill was just the beginning."

"And I couldn't stop it alone."

Another pause.

"I'm not asking you to fix everything. That would be unfair. But I am asking you to finish what I started. Deliver the envelope. Tell Elise the truth. And then… live."

"Not for me. For her."

"For Lila."

The tape clicked to silence.

When I stepped outside, Sam stood immediately.

"Well?" he asked.

"She knew," I said. "All of it. More than we ever guessed."

I held up the envelope.

"Where are we going?" he asked.

"Washington," I said. "The Attorney General's Office."

He blinked. "You're serious."

"If I give this to the press, it becomes a headline. If I give it to the wrong person in town, it disappears. But if I hand this over myself—face to face—it becomes history."

He nodded slowly.

And then we left the vault.

With Eleanor's final weapon.

—

The drive to Washington took four hours.

Elise called midway through.

"You okay?" she asked.

"I'm finishing it," I said. "Really finishing it."

There was a pause.

Then: "Thank you."

—

The AG's office was cold and white and filled with people who did not expect two thirty-somethings carrying a leather-bound ledger and a sealed envelope to walk in unannounced.

But when they saw the names?

When they saw the seal?

When they read the summaries I had prepared?

Everything changed.

Suddenly, I was in a room with federal investigators, handing over files they'd tried and failed to get for decades. Suddenly, I was no longer the niece of a dead woman in a small town—I was a whistleblower. A link in a chain of evidence too thick to ignore.

By the time we left the building, the sky was turning gold with evening.

Sam looked at me as we walked back to the car.

"What now?" he asked.

"I go home," I said. "Back to Rosehill."

"Why?"

"To write it down."

He smiled. "The book?"

I nodded. "It's time to tell it all."

He took my hand.

And we drove back into the twilight.

Back home, I placed the ledger in the drawer of Eleanor's desk—beside her journal. I lit a candle. Opened a new notebook. And began to write.

Not for the courts.

Not for the headlines.

But for the girl who once sat beneath a crooked tree and whispered a name with love.

And for the woman who never stopped saying it aloud.

Chapter 21 The Confession

It arrived in the mail three days after we handed over the ledger.

No return address. No postage mark. Just a plain white envelope tucked into my mailbox—delivered, clearly, by hand.

Inside was a cassette tape.

And a note, typed in a courier font.

"The real story deserves to be heard. Play it. Then decide who should listen next."

At first, I thought it might be a copy of the tape I'd already heard. Eleanor's message to me—the one she left in the safety deposit box.

But it wasn't labeled the same way. No "For Maya." No handwritten signature. Just one word scratched into the plastic in what looked like a nail:

CONFESSION

I didn't wait.

I locked the doors. Pulled the curtains. Sat at Eleanor's desk, with the sun just beginning to dip behind the trees. Then I clicked it into the old tape player and hit PLAY.

The voice that filled the room was Eleanor's.

But it wasn't the tired, reflective voice I'd come to know from her journal or the last tape. This Eleanor sounded sharper. More focused. Alive with fury.

And this time—she wasn't talking to me.

She was talking to a recorder. To evidence. To posterity.

To the truth.

"This is Eleanor Carter. This recording is made on October 2nd, 1991. If you're hearing this, it's because someone finally asked the right question. And someone finally believed me."

"Let me be clear: Lila Carver was pregnant with James Hawthorne's child."

"She told me everything. I remember the night. We were sitting on my porch. She was shaking. Pale. She'd missed her period. Took a test. Showed me the results. And when I asked who the father was… she didn't want to say it. But she didn't deny it when I guessed."

"James had always taken an interest in her. Too much interest. He was her guidance counselor, for God's sake. Twenty-seven. She was seventeen. And he was grooming her. The whole town knew it, in whispers. But no one did anything, because his uncle was on the council. Because his name was Hawthorne."

"She told me James got scared. Said he couldn't be tied to the pregnancy. Said he'd 'fix it' if she didn't disappear. I asked her if she wanted to go to the police. She laughed."

"She said, 'Who would believe me over him?'"

I pressed pause, trembling.

This was it.

Not circumstantial.

Not suggestive.

Direct. Irrefutable.

Eleanor's firsthand account of what Lila told her—delivered in her own voice.

I pressed PLAY again.

"She asked if she could stay with me. Said she just needed a few days to think. To figure out what to do. I said yes. I would've said yes a thousand times over."

"But the next day, when I came home from work, she was gone."

"No note. No bag. No sign of a struggle. But also—no trace."

"And the worst part? They made me question myself. They said she never came to my house. That I was unstable. That I was fabricating things to make the Hawthornes look bad."

"They made me feel insane."

"But I knew."

"I knew what she said. I wrote it down. I recorded this. Because I know someday, someone might come looking. And when they do, they'll need more than memories."

"They'll need a voice."

"So let this be mine."

"Lila was pregnant. James Hawthorne knew. Graham Hawthorne covered it up."

"And someone—maybe them, maybe someone they paid—made her disappear."

"Don't let them win."

"Tell her daughter the truth."

"Tell the town what really happened."

"Tell them I never stopped looking."

"Tell them I never lied."

"This is my confession."

"And my promise."

The tape clicked to silence.

I sat there for a long time, the dusk fading into darkness around me.

No part of me doubted its authenticity.

This was Eleanor—raw and unfiltered. The version of her the town refused to hear. The version that had been labeled crazy, bitter, dangerous.

But all she had been… was right.

This wasn't just a final piece of evidence. It was a weapon.

And it needed to be heard.

The next morning, I made three digital copies.

One went to Jenna. One went to the Attorney General's office.

And one went to Elise.

I drove to her apartment just as the sun was rising, the air crisp and edged with the first bite of late autumn. She answered the door in a sweater and jeans, hair tied back, eyes puffy with sleep.

"I need you to hear this," I said.

We sat on the couch, the file queued on my phone, a Bluetooth speaker humming quietly.

And then Eleanor's voice filled the room.

Elise didn't blink. Didn't speak.

When it ended, she turned to me, tears streaking her cheeks.

"She knew," she whispered. "My whole life… I thought maybe she'd just run. That maybe she didn't love me enough to stay. That maybe… she'd left on her own."

"No," I said gently. "She didn't."

"She tried to fight."

"She did more than fight," I said. "She loved you. Enough to risk everything."

Elise nodded slowly.

Then reached over and took my hand.

"Let's burn the whole lie down."

The press conference was held two days later.

Jenna set it up through a state-level investigative watchdog group. They'd picked up the story after the trial, digging deeper into the financial corruption exposed by the ledger. But now, they had something more powerful than documents.

They had a voice.

Eleanor's.

A woman silenced by an entire town.

Now, heard by thousands.

We played the confession at the opening of the press event.

Journalists didn't blink. They didn't breathe.

They just recorded.

That night, social media exploded.

#JusticeForLila
#EleanorWasRight
#TheWidowSpeaks

Rosehill was in every headline again. But this time, there were no questions. No shadows. Just facts. Eleanor's name—so long treated like a warning—now stood beside Lila's on banners and hashtags and digital billboards.

And Elise?

She stood with me on the courthouse steps.

"I always thought I was born from something shameful," she said to the cameras. "But now I know—I was born from courage. My mother's. And Eleanor's. And now Maya's."

She paused.

"And now I'll carry that story, too."

Back home, I played the tape one last time.

Not for evidence.

Not for justice.

But for her.

For Eleanor.

And when her voice faded, I opened her journal to the final page and wrote five simple words:

"Her confession changed the world."

Chapter 22 The Real Killer

Truth doesn't always arrive with a bang.

Sometimes it comes in whispers.

In broken conversations. In misfiled documents. In faces that don't flinch when they should.

It started with an email from Jenna.

SUBJECT: RE: You were right
Maya—
The AG's office followed up on one of the flagged names in Eleanor's ledger. Cross-referenced a judge's account with phone records, and it led them somewhere new—someone never officially tied to the case.
Check your inbox now. You'll want to sit down.
—J

I opened the attachment.

A scanned affidavit from a former Hawthorne estate staff member. Dated five years ago. Buried in a sealed HR file.

Name redacted.

But the content hit like a thunderclap.

"I was employed by the Hawthorne family from 1984 to 1988. My position required me to handle private errands for both James and Graham Hawthorne. In the summer of 1987, I was asked to deliver an envelope to a man named Randall Grey, who operated out of a cabin near Greenhill Campground. I was told not to ask questions. That it was about 'a girl who needed to disappear.'

"I never saw the girl, but I heard them talk. James was panicking. Said she was pregnant. Said the council would never survive the scandal. Graham told him, quote, 'I'll clean it up, the way I always do.' I heard him say, 'Make sure it looks like she ran. No body. No mess. Just gone.'"

"I left my job shortly after. I was paid to keep quiet. But I never forgot. I knew something terrible had happened."

I read it three times.

Each word carved deeper.

So there it was.

The order.

The cleanup.

The lie.

Lila hadn't run.

She hadn't panicked.

She hadn't changed her mind.

She had been silenced.

And not just by one man. Not just by James. But by Graham—the one who claimed innocence at every turn. The one who smiled for cameras and donated to churches and told Eleanor she was unstable while quietly orchestrating the erasure of a teenage girl and her unborn child.

I forwarded the document to Elise without comment.

A minute later, my phone rang.

She didn't speak at first. Neither did I.

Then:

"They ordered it."

"They did," I said.

"You were right. So was she."

"Elise… there's more. Jenna says Randall Grey never left Rosehill. He changed his name. Opened a garage near the edge of town. Disappeared from public record. But they think he's still here."

"Have they talked to him?"

"They're planning to," I said. "But I want to go first."

Silence.

Then: "I'm coming with you."

We found him at a rundown auto shop just past Route 9, hidden behind a rusted billboard that once advertised fresh cider and Sunday service. The name on the sign read: **"GREYSON AUTO."**

I knew it immediately.

Randall Grey had simply rearranged his shame into a business license.

The bell above the door jingled as we stepped inside.

He looked up from behind the counter.

Older now. Gray-haired, heavy-set, his eyes shadowed with age. But there was a nervousness in him the moment he saw us. A twitch. A shift in posture. Recognition.

"You don't look like you need a tire rotation," he said, voice low.

"No," I said. "We're here for a different kind of alignment."

His gaze narrowed. "You're Carter's niece."

"And she was right about you."

His face froze.

"I don't know what you think—"

"You delivered the envelope," I interrupted. "You were told to make her disappear."

"I didn't touch that girl," he said quickly.

"But you knew what was going to happen," I said. "And you helped anyway."

Elise stepped forward, her voice shaking.

"Her name was Lila Carver. She was seventeen. She was pregnant. She trusted someone she shouldn't have. And she died because of it. Because of men like you."

He looked at her—really looked. And something in him cracked.

"You're hers."

"Yes," she said. "And I'm here to make sure she's never hidden again."

He sank onto the stool behind the counter.

"You don't understand what it was like back then," he said. "The Hawthornes owned everything. Everyone owed them something. I was just trying to keep my job."

"You did more than keep your job," I said. "You helped cover up a murder."

He swallowed hard.

"I didn't kill her," he said again, like a prayer. "I just… I dropped off the money. I didn't know what they'd do. When I heard later that she'd gone missing, I… I just shut it down. I pretended I didn't know."

"But you did," I said. "And now you're going to say it. On the record."

He looked up at us, sweat glistening on his forehead.

"If I do… they'll come for me."

"No," I said. "They won't. Because we already did."

I turned and gestured toward the window.

Two plainclothes officers stepped out of an unmarked car. They approached slowly, nodding at us, then at Grey.

"This is your chance," I said. "Tell the truth. For once."

Grey looked at Elise again.

Then nodded.

And finally—after three decades of silence—he spoke.

The statement he gave that day was enough to open a new investigation.

With Grey's testimony, and Eleanor's recordings, and the financial trail leading directly to campaign funds and state contributions— Graham Hawthorne's legal walls crumbled like ash.

He was re-indicted within the week.

This time, not just for obstruction.

But for conspiracy to commit murder.

James was never found.

But that didn't matter anymore.

The truth had risen.

And it was loud.

—

On the eve of the new trial, I stood beneath the crooked tree at Greenhill.

The bark had worn with time, the symbol Eleanor carved now barely visible. But it still hummed with memory.

I traced the lines with my fingers.

"I found her," I whispered.

Not a body.

But the truth.

That was enough.

Elise stepped beside me and set a photograph at the base of the tree. Lila, smiling. Seventeen. Alive.

"She didn't run," Elise said.

"No," I said. "She was silenced."

"But not anymore."

We stood in the quiet for a while.

Then we left the photograph behind.

A marker.

A monument.

A promise.

Chapter 23 A Trusted Betrayal

Trust, I've learned, doesn't break like glass. It erodes—slowly, silently—until one day you reach for it, and your hand closes on dust.

I never imagined it would be Sam.

Not him.

Not after everything.

Not after the woods, the tapes, the trial, the promises whispered under a starless sky.

But now, I see it—the cracks I ignored. The moments too carefully orchestrated. The way he always seemed to know just enough, always had the right tool, the next contact, the right phrase to calm me down when the truth got too close.

He never led me away from the truth.

But he made sure I stayed just far enough not to destroy the whole thing.

Until now.

—

It started with a phone call from Jenna.

"I need to talk to you," she said. "In person. Now."

She sounded tight, strained—like something was pulling her apart from the inside.

An hour later, we sat across from each other in her office, the blinds drawn.

She placed a file on the desk between us.

"What is this?" I asked.

"It's everything I never wanted to believe," she said.

I opened the folder.

And my world tilted.

Inside were copies of emails, encrypted text threads, bank logs—nothing explosive at first glance. But the deeper I read, the tighter my chest became.

Because they weren't addressed to Graham Hawthorne.

They were addressed to someone else.

Samuel J. Wilcox.

Dates ranging back a year before I came to Rosehill. Communications with Graham's shell organizations. Updates on Eleanor's investigation. And most damning—payments. Small ones. Disguised. But consistent.

"The money was funneled through a dummy consultancy," Jenna said softly. "It's buried under multiple layers, but the final deposit lands in an account Sam opened last spring."

"No," I said. "No, there's no way."

"I didn't want to believe it either."

"He's the one who got hurt. He nearly died."

"Or he made sure he looked like a target. To stay close. To guide what you saw."

My hands clenched around the papers.

"I don't understand. Why would he do this?"

"Because sometimes betrayal doesn't look like silence," Jenna said. "Sometimes it looks like support. Like being the perfect ally—until it matters most."

—

I drove home in silence.

The world blurred outside my windshield, but inside, everything sharpened into a point. I was replaying every moment—every shared look, every midnight theory session, every time he said "I believe you."

Was it true?

Had any of it been?

The house was dark when I arrived.

I unlocked the door and stepped inside slowly.

"Sam?" I called.

No answer.

The living room was empty.

But the light in Eleanor's study was on.

I walked toward it.

And there he was.

Sitting at her desk.

The journal open in front of him.

He didn't turn when I entered.

"You went through her files again," I said.

"I needed to see something," he said softly.

"You mean you needed to check if she left anything else behind. Anything you didn't catch."

Now he turned.

His expression wasn't guilty.

It was… resigned.

"Maya, I can explain."

"Don't," I said. "Don't insult either of us."

He stood slowly. "It wasn't supposed to be like this."

"Then what was it supposed to be?"

He swallowed. "I was approached by Graham over a year ago. Before I even met you. Before Eleanor died. They knew Eleanor was getting close to something. They wanted someone near her. Someone quiet. Someone trusted."

"And you said yes."

"I said maybe," he said. "I didn't agree to everything. Just to… watch. To keep tabs. I didn't expect her to die. I didn't expect to care."

I stepped back.

"You lied to me."

"I didn't lie," he said. "I left things out. But I never misled you. Not really."

"You pretended to fight with me. You held me when I cried. You helped me bury evidence. Was that all part of the plan?"

"No," he said. "That was the part I didn't expect."

I laughed bitterly.

"You think that makes it better?"

"I tried to stop," he said. "But it was too late. And then Graham got arrested. The case exploded. And suddenly I was in deeper than I could dig myself out."

"And the payments?" I asked. "Those just showed up on their own?"

He looked down. "I took them at first. For information. But I stopped after Eleanor died."

"Except you didn't stop," I said. "You kept taking. And you kept lying."

He looked up then, his eyes sharp.

"I was trying to protect you."

"From what?"

"From burning yourself alive chasing ghosts."

I stepped forward, fury rising in my throat.

"Those ghosts were people. Lila. Eleanor. Elise's mother. You helped the people who destroyed them. And now you want me to believe you cared?"

He said nothing.

I reached for the flash drive on the desk—the one with Eleanor's recordings, the ledger, the documents he'd asked to "help back up."

He reached at the same time.

Our hands collided.

I moved faster.

I pulled the drive from the port and stepped back.

"You don't get to have this," I said. "Not anymore."

"Maya," he said. "Please."

I stared at him.

And saw the truth.

He wasn't a monster.

He was something worse.

He was a coward.

And I had trusted him with everything.

I turned and walked out of the study, out of the house, out into the cold night.

He didn't follow me.

I stayed with Jenna for the next two nights.

We backed up the drive. Transferred every file to three separate encrypted servers.

Then we sent the full documentation of Sam's involvement to the AG's office.

"I don't know if they'll charge him," Jenna said. "It's murky. And they'll want to keep the focus on Graham."

"That's fine," I said. "I'm not here for vengeance."

"Then what do you want?"

I looked at her.

"Closure."

Elise asked to meet me under the tree.

The one where it all began.

We stood in silence for a long time.

Then she said, "You loved him."

"I thought I did."

"He helped you get here."

"And nearly helped bury it again," I said.

She nodded. "People betray us for different reasons. Fear. Shame. Greed. But it doesn't mean the truth dies."

"No," I said. "It means we fight harder to keep it alive."

Later that night, I returned to Eleanor's desk alone.

I picked up her pen.

And on the last blank page of her journal, I wrote:

"The hardest part of truth is realizing it doesn't always come from your enemies. Sometimes, it bleeds from the wounds left by those who swore to hold you."

"But even betrayal cannot erase the past."

"It only makes the telling of it more necessary."

Chapter 24 The Exposure

It began with a ping.

One simple notification. A story sent to my phone.

BREAKING: Rosehill Scandal Widens – Secret Recordings Implicate Council in 1987 Disappearance

And then another.

Eleanor Carter's Tapes Go Public — "I Never Lied" Becomes Rallying Cry

And another.

Whistleblower Journal Sparks National Probe Into Judicial Corruption

Each alert struck like lightning. And each one was a thunderclap Eleanor never got to hear.

But I did.

I was sitting on the back porch of her house—my house now—when it hit me all at once: the story was out. It wasn't ours anymore. It belonged to the world.

Everything we had unearthed—Eleanor's recordings, the ledger, Lila's letter, Grey's testimony—was now in the hands of journalists, legal analysts, documentarians, and most importantly: the people.

And they were listening.

The fire we'd lit in secret now burned across every screen in America.

Jenna's phone call came an hour later.

"We did it," she said, breathless.

"Are they running it on-air?"

"CNN. MSNBC. The Times is leading their Sunday issue with a feature on Eleanor's journal. The whole thing. Her love story with Lila. The Hawthorne empire. Elise."

I stood, the wind hitting my face like a baptism.

"Did they play the tape?"

"Yes. The entire confession. No edits."

My chest tightened. "She's finally being heard."

"They're calling it the Widow's Voice," Jenna said. "Hashtag's already trending."

I laughed softly. "She would've hated that."

"She would've corrected the grammar," Jenna said, and we both smiled through the silence.

Then she added, "I'm proud of you."

I swallowed hard. "She would be too."

—

By noon, my inbox was full.

Requests for interviews. Invitations to speak at conferences. A woman from a publishing house wanted to discuss turning the story into a memoir. A documentary team offered to come to Rosehill and film on location.

I ignored most of them.

This wasn't a spectacle.

It was a reckoning.

But I knew one thing: I needed to speak. Not to capitalize. Not to sell. But to honor.

So when the journalist from The Washington Post called, I said yes.

Her name was Anika Sethi. Calm, focused, and deeply respectful. She flew in that Friday.

We met at the crooked tree.

"I thought we'd do the interview here," I said. "It's where the truth was buried."

"And now it's where it blooms," she replied, setting up her voice recorder.

She asked about Eleanor. About Lila. About what it felt like to dig through decades of silence and finally make the town listen.

I answered honestly.

"It wasn't easy. Eleanor was labeled paranoid. Lila was erased. The men who destroyed them were respected, protected. But the truth doesn't disappear just because no one looks for it. It waits."

"And when did you know you had to tell it?"

"When I realized it wasn't just their story. It was mine too."

"And how does it feel now, to have the truth out in the open?"

I looked around at the trees. The shifting light. The breeze that carried the weight of names too long unsaid.

"It feels like mourning and justice shaking hands."

—

The article ran that Sunday.

**"The Widow's Journal: One Woman's Fight to Unbury a
Town's Darkest Secret"**
By Anika Sethi

It was poetic, raw, factual without being cold. She didn't
sensationalize. She humanized. Eleanor's words were quoted.
Lila's letter reprinted in full. Elise's story framed as a miracle—not
of survival, but of resurrection.

And I, for once, was not the center.

Just the thread.

The girl who followed a woman's ghost and found another's voice.

—

The response was overwhelming.

Letters arrived at the house from across the country. Survivors.
Witnesses. Daughters of women who had been silenced in other
towns, other eras.

One woman wrote:

**"Eleanor gave me courage. Lila gave me clarity. You gave me
the reason to speak."**

Another:

**"I never thought truth could win. Thank you for proving it
can."**

And still another:

"For the first time, my daughter believes me."

I read every one.

Cried over more than I could count.

But it was Elise's call that undid me.

"They sent flowers," she said.

"Who did?"

"The school board. The same board that fired Eleanor. They sent a public apology. A wreath. A statement calling her brave."

My throat tightened. "She never got to hear it."

"But I did," Elise whispered. "And my son will too."

—

The town of Rosehill changed.

Slowly. Uneasily.

But undeniably.

The Hawthorne name was stripped from the town square. Their estate was frozen, turned over for investigation. Graham's retrial was fast-tracked.

A small plaque was installed outside the courthouse.

**In memory of Eleanor Carter and Lila Carver.
For the truths we buried, and those who unearthed them.**

I stood beside Elise when they unveiled it.

She wore her mother's necklace.

I wore Eleanor's pin.

Neither of us spoke.

We didn't have to.

The silence was sacred now.

Not a hiding place.

But a moment of recognition.

—

The final interview I gave was for a podcast.

Not a national outlet.

Just a quiet, thoughtful show called *Echoes in the Dark*, hosted by a journalist named Rayna who had followed the case from the beginning.

"I want to ask something different," she said. "Not about the evidence. Or the men. But about Eleanor."

"Okay," I said.

"What do you think she'd say, seeing all this now?"

I paused.

Looked out the window.

Smiled.

"She'd ask why it took so damn long."

Rayna laughed.

"And then?"

"She'd pour tea. Sit down. And start writing the next chapter."

—

That night, I lit a candle for Eleanor.

Placed it on the windowsill.

Then I sat at her desk and opened a fresh journal.

The first line I wrote:

"Truth doesn't rot. It ripens."

And I kept writing.

For Lila.

For Eleanor.

For Elise.

For myself.

For every woman who ever screamed into silence and waited for an echo.

This was the echo.

And it would never go quiet again.

Chapter 25 Aftermath

The courtroom was full, but the silence inside it was absolute.

The second Hawthorne trial didn't have the same spectacle as the first. There were no networks swarming the courthouse steps. No frenzied reporters. No chaos.

This time, there was only gravity.

Graham Hawthorne stood in his navy suit, older now, his legacy in tatters. His defense team was thinner. His confidence—what little remained—was brittle.

And this time, he wasn't being accused of corruption.

He was being charged with conspiracy to commit murder.

Grey's testimony. Eleanor's tapes. The ledger. Lila's letter. All of it, piece by piece, made into a mosaic the jury couldn't look away from.

When the verdict came, it wasn't just legal.

It was spiritual.

Guilty.

Not just for what he did.

But for what he tried to erase.

I stood beside Elise on the steps afterward, reporters snapping photos from a respectful distance. She looked poised, strong.

"I wish she could've seen it," I said softly.

"She did," Elise said. "She just saw it through us."

That night, we lit two candles. One for Lila.

And one for Eleanor.

They flickered side by side in the courtroom window.

For the first time, not in mourning.

But in victory.

—

Clearing Eleanor's name was easier than I expected.

Jenna drafted the request to the town council. I attached Eleanor's full journal and transcripts from the confession. The council convened quietly, but unanimously passed the motion.

The public record was updated.

Eleanor Carter's termination was reversed.

Her name was posthumously honored with a commendation from the state for "exceptional civic vigilance in the pursuit of truth."

It was symbolic.

But it mattered.

Her grave received a new headstone:

Eleanor M. Carter
1947–2023
Teacher. Truth-teller. Guardian of the forgotten.
"She never stopped looking."

Elise and I stood over it in the cold morning light, the autumn wind whispering through the pine trees.

"She was never just 'The Widow,'" I said.

"No," Elise replied. "She was the light in the dark."

—

I stayed in Rosehill.

I told myself I would leave when the book was done.

Then I told myself I'd leave once the documentary aired.

Then I stopped lying to myself.

This was home now.

Not because it had always been good.

But because it had been redeemed.

Because we made it honest.

The house needed repairs. The wallpaper was peeling in places. Some floorboards still groaned like old ghosts.

But I loved it.

Every creak. Every shadow.

It felt less like I was living in Eleanor's house.

And more like she had made space in it for me.

—

I called the book *The Widow's Last Secret*.

And I started it with a question.

"What do we owe the dead?"

The answer, I discovered, was not silence.

It was voice.

It was legacy.

It was light.

The book took six months to write. Another three to edit. The publisher wanted to change the ending—"less melancholy," they said. "More hopeful."

I refused.

Because endings, I told them, aren't meant to be neat.

Especially when the dead still whisper.

—

The night before the manuscript was due, I sat at Eleanor's desk and pulled open the drawer I hadn't touched in weeks.

Inside was her journal.

The original.

I opened it, flipping to the final page.

My handwriting stared back at me:

"It only makes the telling of it more necessary."

And beneath it—

A faint, almost imperceptible indentation in the paper.

I ran my fingers over it.

It wasn't my handwriting.

It wasn't Eleanor's.

I turned the page.

The back of the paper had a barely visible phrase etched into it.

As if someone had written it on the page before, pressed hard, then torn the top sheet off.

I held it to the light.

My blood ran cold.

It said:

"They got to her."

—

At first, I thought it had to be a mistake.

Old ink bleed?

My own scribbling, reversed?

But it was too deliberate.

Too intentional.

And it wasn't in Eleanor's handwriting.

It was shakier. Tighter.

Like someone writing fast.

Or in fear.

I tore through the journal. Page after page. Margin notes. Loose ends.

And then, tucked inside the back cover—under the lining—I found a slip of paper.

An autopsy request.

Signed by Jenna.

Stamped **UNOFFICIAL COPY**.

My heart raced.

I called her immediately.

"Jenna. Did you authorize a second look at Eleanor's death?"

There was silence.

Then, "I was going to tell you after the verdict."

"What did they find?"

She took a breath.

"There were inconsistencies."

"Like what?"

"She was found slumped over her desk. You saw the photos. It looked like a stroke. Natural causes. But the toxicology report…"

"What?"

"She had traces of digitalis."

My breath caught.

"Foxglove?"

"Yes. Enough to mimic heart failure. Enough to kill her slowly."

"Are you saying she was poisoned?"

"I'm saying someone made it look like her heart stopped. But it didn't stop on its own."

I sat down, the room spinning.

"You're sure?"

"I had a second pathologist confirm it. Quietly. It's not official, but…"

I closed my eyes.

"They got to her."

"I'm sorry, Maya."

I thought back to that last entry.

To Eleanor's final recording.

To her last line.

"Tell them I never lied."

And now, I knew why she'd said it with such urgency.

Because she knew the end was coming.

And not from natural causes.

The police reopened the case.

Quietly.

Discreetly.

No press. No leaks.

The files are still classified.

The town doesn't know yet.

Maybe they never will.

But I know.

And I wrote it down.

On the final page of the manuscript, I added a postscript:

POSTSCRIPT
Months after this book was completed, a medical review of Eleanor Carter's death revealed traces of digitalis, a lethal toxin derived from the foxglove plant, in her system at levels consistent with induced cardiac arrest.

Her death, long ruled natural, is now under renewed investigation by state authorities.

We may never know who administered the dose, or when. But one thing is clear:

She didn't die quietly.
She died fighting.
And even then, she left behind the truth.

When the publisher read it, they called me.

"Are you sure you want to include this?" the editor asked. "It casts a dark cloud."

"It shines a light," I said.

And we kept it.

—

On the one-year anniversary of Eleanor's death, I stood under the crooked tree with Elise.

We said nothing.

Just left two roses.

One white.

One red.

Then I placed a copy of the book beneath the roots.

Wrapped in plastic.

Marked only by a symbol Eleanor had carved decades earlier.

A crescent.

And a cross.

Back home, I lit the final candle on the windowsill.

Watched it flicker.

Watched the fog curl around the edges of the garden like memory.

Then I returned to the desk.

A new journal sat open.

Blank.

Waiting.

And I began to write again.

Not the story of Eleanor.

Not the story of Lila.

Not even my own.

But the next one.

Because some truths never stop whispering.

And someone must always listen.